Life Goes On

By

Kimberly R. Bartley

Hilary,
Always
hold onto
Rom 8:28
Kimberly
Bartley

Chapter One

"Remember when we first met?" Dexter reasoned. "Remember that little cafe?"

Sarah turned to face him, standing with her hands on her hips. An oppositional pose if he'd ever seen one. It was very appropriate, he thought. It matched the tone of the past few weeks, maybe months. When *did* all this start? Dexter couldn't even remember now. This opposition, unfortunately, felt like their new normal. He struggled to remember the happy times, and he *knew* Sarah had lost sight of them. A Godly friend had once counseled him to understand that there was an ebb and flow to the marital relationship and not to expect it to be all sunshine and roses. When he had asked how to get through the rough patches, his friend, Anthony, had told him to revisit the reasons he had fallen in love to begin with, to be intentional about remembering the happier times and to hold onto that when things were sour. That's what Dexter was trying to do. And he was trying to urge Sarah to remember right along with him. Judging from her stance, she was apparently having nothing to do with it.

"Why do you do that?" she finally said.

"Do *what*?" he asked, befuddled.

"Try to pretend nothing's wrong!"

Dexter blew out a sigh, trying not to feel defeated. "Well, for one thing -- I can't seem to get to the bottom of what's wrong." And that was the truth. He couldn't get to the core issue. All he knew was that nothing he did pleased her. Everything he did seemed to be wrong. "And another thing -- what's wrong with trying to stay in touch with all the things that are *right* about us? Don't you remember how it felt to love me? Can't we try to find that again?"

"Oh for goodness sake, Dex! Do you really think it's that simple?" She was exasperated with him. And *he* was frustrated with the situation. Another deep breath before he trusted himself to speak. He didn't want to fight. He was willing to do his part to resolve their issues, whatever they were.

"I don't think it has to be that complicated," he said softly, taking a step closer to her.

"Just don't," she commanded firmly.

Dexter put his hands up in surrender. He was at a loss as to how to proceed. All he knew to do was pray, and he'd spent time doing that already. Anthony had been a great sounding board, but Dexter had kept things general when they'd discussed it. It was humiliating to admit that his wife seemed to have simply fallen out of love with him. Besides, all the advice in the world wouldn't help when only one was willing to try and save the marriage. And that certainly seemed to be the case here. No matter what Dexter tried to do, it seemed that Sarah was unhappy. He loved her, and his heart was breaking. She had built a hard shell of bitterness around herself that he couldn't manage to penetrate. He just couldn't find his Sarah that loved him back.

It was difficult not to resent other happy couples. His own brother, who loved his wife but had a wandering eye, possessed the devotion of his spouse in spite of his imperfections. And there was Anthony and Christina, who seemed to have the perfect marriage. What was *he* doing wrong?!

Dexter retreated, leaving Sarah standing in the kitchen alone with her acrimony. He went into the garage and busied himself with getting his tools in order for an odd job for a fellow church member. That task took up a couple of hours of his afternoon. Maybe Sarah would have cooled down by the time he got back. His optimism warmed as he pictured going in with a plan to order takeout and watch a movie. He just had to stay at it, right? He had to convince her that they were worth fighting for. He was willing to go the extra mile. That's what marriage was all about. There might be another time when Sarah would be the one putting in more effort. Dexter was encouraged, his resolve strengthened. He was even whistling when he came through the door.

Catching sight of two boxes and Sarah's suitcase at the bottom of the stairs silenced his tune and halted his steps. She had threatened to leave before, had hinted at a separation -- but nothing had been said recently. Dexter was completely blindsided by the scene before him. Just then, she came down the steps with a large duffel bag slung over her shoulder. She paused when she realized he was home. Their eyes locked, his imploring, hers defiant. "This is for the best," she stated simply, shouldering past him.

Dexter was speechless. Chivalrous by nature, it was unlike him to watch someone -- especially a woman, especially his *wife* -- carry a load without offering to help. In this case, however, it was beyond him to offer his assistance as his wife left him. Instead, he stood by watching Sarah load up her vehicle and drive off. He was unable to find words to ask questions or reason with her. He had no idea where she was going or what would happen next.

She would have her cell phone though. Maybe after she'd had time to settle down they could talk. He would give her a little time to miss him before he called. Absence makes the heart grow fonder -- that's what people always say. Maybe some good *could* come out of a temporary separation. He kept telling himself that while he went through the motions of living. He ordered takeout, but was only able to eat a few bites of it. He flipped through the channels on the television, but never settled on anything that would hold his attention. He answered a text message from his brother, Spencer, who invited him to join him and Anthony for 18 holes the next day. He agreed to go, knowing he needed to get out of the house, but couldn't even work up any enthusiasm for the lemonade Anthony's wife would likely send.

Before going to bed, Dexter finally caved and sent a text message to Sarah. **At least lmk ur safe.**

There was no reply for a solid ten minutes, and then only **I'm fine.**

He didn't bother with a reply. It was obvious that she didn't want to engage in a conversation. *Give her a chance to miss you,* he reminded himself, turning off the light. He tried to pray, but had to count on the Romans 8 promise of intercession because the words just wouldn't come. All he managed was, "Father, stay close to me. Keep Your hand on my marriage." He uttered an amen and allowed the fitful sleep of the weary to pull him under.

Chapter Two

Those initial hours without Sarah -- the ones where Dexter just went through the motions of living -- turned into days. And then those days turned into weeks, and the weeks turned into months. The entire span of time went by with only perfunctory communication between him and Sarah. She was through with their marriage, and offered no hope of reconciliation. He had tried on multiple occasions to reconnect, to rekindle. Sarah was not receptive.

Dexter had a pretty good support system, but was so embarrassed about the whole situation that he hadn't made use of it. He had shared with Anthony that he and Sarah were having problems, but he had been pretty vague. And he had never told anyone outside the family that they were separated. In fact, he had confided only in Spencer and his wife, along with his sister, Blaire, out of necessity. They would question Sarah's absence at family events. They had been supportive, but it was still hard for him to discuss. His church family would have been supportive, too, but he had skirted questions and made excuses for her absence. He visited other churches frequently to camouflage her disappearance.

And then one day, he received notification that she had filed for divorce. Dexter was devastated. He wasn't surprised, but he was crushed. He felt like such a failure for not being able to hold his marriage together. He questioned himself, reflecting on everything he could recall that could have contributed to its demise. In fact, he nearly drove himself crazy analyzing every little thing. So when the papers came, it was then that he realized he probably needed to have a conversation with his pastor.

This turned out to be a smart move. The pastor helped put things back in perspective and take the shame out of the situation. Dexter intended to be married all his life though, and knew that was the way God meant for it to be. "But God hates divorce. Doesn't it say so in the Bible?"

"You're talking about the verse in Malachi," Pastor James replied. "I would agree that divorce goes against God's plan for marriage, and I believe His word verifies this. *But* a marriage is *two* people and you are just one person. You are responsible for your part in it, and Sarah is responsible for hers. Now, I'm not judging Sarah -- her actions are between her and God -- but from what you've shared, it sounds like you've done everything you can."

"I was committed to our marriage," he said, adding, "I would have never chosen this."

"I believe that. And God knows your heart. All you can do now is move on from here."

"I'm trying," Dexter offered.

"Come back next week," Pastor James said, "Let's talk some more."

Dexter agreed to return for another session the following weekend. He chided himself for waiting so long before seeking counsel. He felt like a weight had been lifted from his chest. He couldn't help but wonder if his marriage might have survived if Sarah had agreed to counseling when he had suggested it. There was no point in wondering "what if?" though.

Throughout the week, Dexter really began to own the fact that he had done everything he could do, that this was Sarah's choice, that it was truly over. And surprisingly, when he let go of all the guilt and shame he'd been feeling, he realized that his pride was wounded, but his heart wasn't exactly broken. It was true that he wouldn't have chosen to end their marriage, but it had been a very long time since he and Sarah had been in a good place. He missed them as the couple they had been five years ago, and he missed having someone… but he wasn't sure he missed *her*. Not like he was supposed to. What did that mean?

Dexter pondered this, and was eager to speak with Pastor James on Saturday afternoon. When he arrived for his appointment, however, the church secretary told him that the pastor had been called out to help out with a situation a sister church was facing while its pastor dealt with the sudden death of one of its members. Disappointed, he rescheduled and whispered a prayer for the family affected by this death.

It wasn't until several hours later that word trickled down the grapevine that it was his own friend, Anthony, who had passed suddenly of an apparent heart attack. Tony! They had just golfed together a few days back! Poor Christina. Dexter could hardly wrap his mind around it, and could only imagine how Tony's family must be feeling. What a terrible loss! Anthony Sinclair was one of the best men he knew. He wished he could do something, but felt so helpless. So he did all he knew to do at the moment … he commenced to praying that God would comfort the family and that God would show him how to help.

~~~~~~~~~

Dexter, of course, stopped by the funeral home to pay his respects. Christina was gracious and polite, but he had the sense that she was moving on autopilot. He wondered how much of these terrible days she would remember later. After speaking with her for a moment, he took an inconspicuous seat in the back of the room. From there, he watched as Christina and her children greeted people and exchanged lamentations. She seemed to lean heavily on them, and he was glad that she had them.

Sarah had never really wanted children, and he hadn't pushed for them. Now though, watching the solidarity with which Anthony's family faced their grief, it occurred to him that he would never know that kind of comfort during a tragedy. Indeed, he had faced his recent version of tragedy -- the end of his marriage -- with very little support. Of course, kids would have just complicated that particular situation. He supposed it was a different kind of loss, but it was certainly one he had grieved. A familiar voice pulled him from his reverie.

It was Anthony and Christina's oldest son, Jordan. "Dexter?"

Dexter stood quickly, extending a hand and pulling Jordan into an embrace. "Hey, man," he said, "I was so sorry to hear about your dad."

"I know," Jordan said, pulling back to look the older man in the eye. "It caught us all off guard."

"How's everyone holding up?"

"Okay, I think. It's hard to tell. I think it's still settling in on us… you know, in degrees."

"I can only imagine," Dexter offered. "What can I do? Is there any way I can help?"

"Nothing that I know of," Jordan replied. "Just keep us in your prayers."

"Of course. Always."

A beautiful young lady approached just then. Jordan placed an arm around her waist in a lovingly possessive manner. "Dex, have you met my bride? This is Brianna," he said, and then to his wife, "Honey, this is Dexter. He's a brother to our neighbor and a friend of Dad's."

"It's a pleasure to meet you, Brianna."

"Likewise," she said, then to Jordan, "We need to get your mom to eat something."

Jordan promised to come along and check on his mother, but turned back to Dexter once more. "Dad thought a lot of you, Dex. Thank you so much for being here."

"Your dad was a great man. It was an honor to call him my friend. Please give me a call if there's anything you guys need. You will, won't you?"

"Sure will," Jordan said, firmly shaking his hand again in parting.

Dexter sought out Haley and Payton, the other Sinclair children, before leaving. He offered condolences, but hardly knew what to say at such a time. They were so young. Payton hadn't even graduated from high school yet. So many milestones Tony would miss, he thought sadly. He bumped into Justin and Brent, two of Tony's good friends, on his way out. They commiserated for a moment about how much Anthony Sinclair would be missed.

When Dexter returned the next day, he took a seat next to his brother and sister-in-law. The service was a tasteful celebration of Anthony's life. He was a man who knew Jesus as a friend and savior, so he knew there was reason to celebrate. But the human side of us wants what it wants -- in this case, our friend/spouse/father here with us. And so the service held sorrow as well. Some were sticking around for a meal that had been prepared for the family, but he did not. Just before he left, he spoke with his sister-in-law, Paula. "Let me know if there's any way I can help the family," he said, jerking his head in the direction of the bereft Sinclairs. She agreed that she would.

He left, not knowing what else to do. Dexter had been forced to learn how to live without Sarah. Now, Christina would have to learn how to go on without Tony. That's one thing he had found to be true -- even when the unimaginable happens, life goes on for the living.

Chapter Three

Pastor James greeted Dexter with a hearty handshake. "Come on in," he said, welcoming the younger man into his study. "How have you been?"

"Well, better in many ways," Dexter said as he took a seat to the side of the pastor's desk. "But honestly, still reeling from the loss of a friend."

"Ah, you mean Anthony Sinclair," he said thoughtfully. "Tough stuff, losing someone so suddenly."

"Yeah, it sure is. I'll never play a round of golf without thinking of him."

"A common interest?" the older man asked.

"Yes, we've played countless times. I didn't spend a lot of time with him outside of the golf course, but I had met his family. Great people. I just can't stop thinking about them."

"A loss is never easy, but from all accounts, Sinclair was a good man who knew the Lord. That's a comfort. It is very fitting that you should continue to play golf and that you remember him every single time."

Dexter drew in a breath and exhaled slowly. "I guess you're right."

"Have you had any contact with Sarah since we last spoke?" the pastor asked.

"No, she seldom answers my texts. She seems content without me in her life so I've quit trying to be in it."

"Has that been difficult?"

"It was at first, but you know…" Dexter paused, putting his thoughts in order before continuing, "since I've let go of the guilt and shame I'd been carrying around, I've really...well, not been *okay* with it... but I've had a *peace* about it."

"I'm glad to hear that, Dexter. I believe that the enemy sometimes uses our emotions and even our desire to do right to paralyze us. He reminds us of our mistakes or imperfections and it keeps us from moving forward in God's service sometimes."

"I can see that. I feel like the Lord had been healing my heart because...," Dexter said, hesitating to give voice to what he'd been feeling. Pastor James' silence urged him on. "Even though I wouldn't have chosen for my marriage to end, I'm not brokenhearted like I thought."

"Ah, well," the pastor offered, "Perhaps that is His assurance that this valley was necessary in order for you to get to a place where you'll be ready for His next blessing."

"Surely this whole travesty was not part of His will..."

"I'm not suggesting that," clarified Pastor James. "But you know as well as I do that God allows us free will. *And* that He uses even the bad to bring about good. I'm prone to believe that every bit of adversity we face prepares our hearts for greater things."

"I hope you're right," Dexter said with a chuckle. "And you probably are -- God is awfully good!"

"That He is!" Pastor James agreed.

After a heartfelt prayer, led by the pastor, that offered praise for God's goodness, asked that the enemy be bound from any foothold in Dexter's situation, and beseeched God's healing and comfort for the Sinclair family, Dexter left the pastor's study in much improved spirits. He whispered another prayer of thanksgiving as he walked out into the sunlight, for he was very grateful for God's obedient servants who kept him grounded.

Dexter had a couple of errands to run, and then planned to head over to his sister's house. Blair was a single woman and fiercely independent. She had come close to marrying at one point, but broke it off after a one year engagement. Dexter never could get to the bottom of her decision, but suspected that it had something to do with seeing some warning signs in him that they all wondered if Paula hadn't seen in their brother, Spencer. Spencer would never say anything inappropriate in front of his wife, but being a man himself, Dexter could see the way he sized women up when he encountered them. He appraised them like a jeweler appraises a gemstone. How he followed up was anyone's guess, but neither Dexter nor Blair would have been surprised if there had been infidelities. Could Paula really not see?

Blair was younger than her brothers, coming along well after their parents had given up on having a little girl. But everything in God's time, right? And she had been such a blessing to their family. Spencer was the oldest, and for ten years it was just the two boys. Then Blair was born and all the animosity between the brothers shifted into a common purpose. They became the doting big brothers to their baby sister. Spencer and Dexter dropped whatever sibling rivalry they might have had going on to become Blair's protector as she grew up -- until she hit about seventeen and shrugged them off like an unneeded jacket on a warm afternoon in May. Once she returned from college, Blair was well on her way to independence. But it was after her breakup with Oliver that she seemed to develop this determination that she wouldn't rely on anyone else. She was the queen of youtube tutorials and do-it-yourself projects. So when she called to invite Dexter over for dinner and mentioned a plumbing issue that she couldn't get a handle on, he knew it was major.

Two hours later found him and Blair working shoulder to shoulder under her bathroom sink. They wrestled pipes and passed tools back and forth, and soon zeroed in on the problem. Once they found the problem, they were able to conquer it. Dexter got to his feet and washed his hands. "When can we eat? I'm starving."

"The roast should be ready anytime now. Smells good, doesn't it?"

"Sure does," he said.

"I'll go check on it," she said. Wagging a finger at the array of tools on the floor, she admonished, "You clean up your mess."

"*My* mess?" he asked with mock indignance.

Blair only laughed, disappearing down the hall. Dexter tidied up the area where they had been working and washed his hands thoroughly. When he emerged from the bathroom, tools packed back into his toolbox, the aroma was even stronger than before. His mouth watered. He set the toolbox down near the back door, and went to hover in the kitchen like their childhood pet, a sweet mutt named Scruffy, used to do -- just hoping for a bite. "Could I just get a little taste?" he asked, reaching around Blair toward the roast.

She smacked his hand promptly, and held a meat fork up in a playfully threatening gesture. "Just hold your horses!" she admonished. "Hand me a couple of plates."

Dexter did as he was told, and while she plated up the dinner, poured himself a glass of milk. "Want some?" he asked, holding up the jug. Blair answered in the affirmative, and he obliged her. She set the plates on the table. The one in front of him was mounded up with a generous portion of beef, carrots, and potatoes. Dexter led the quickest blessing in history and dove in. "Mmm, Blair, you are such a good cook!"

"Go ahead," she said with a smirk. "Finish the sentence the way everyone else does."

When he looked up in confusion, she elaborated theatrically, "'Oh, Blair, you're such a good cook. It's a shame that you live alone and have no one to cook for!' Or how 'bout this one? 'You'll make somebody a good wife someday.'"

Dexter chuckled. "Well, I don't think it's a shame at all. Especially when *I* reap the benefits!" He paused, and then added, "I *do* think you would make a great wife though, if that's what you want. I'm a little biased, I know, but I believe a man would be blessed to have you."

She smiled. "I don't know if that's what the Lord has in store for me or not," she said. "I'm not exactly a spring chicken, you know."

"Hey," Dexter said sharply. "Thirty-six is *not* old!"

"No, but *forty*-six is!" she countered.

"Here, I'm trying to be nice and you have to cut on my age."

"I'm just teasing," she soothed, and then turned serious. "You know I'm okay either way, right?"

"Yes, I know."

"I'm content. And I don't want a man just for the sake of having a man. I'm happy on my own, and if the Lord doesn't have someone in mind for me, that'll be just fine."

Dexter nodded thoughtfully and continued eating. He admired her. He couldn't seem to get to that place of contentment. He longed for a help meet, and felt adrift without someone with whom to share his life. Blair truly seemed content without someone -- it wasn't just lip service. Maybe God had a different call on her life. Maybe that was why there was a longing in his heart.

He tucked those thoughts away and focused on the evening at hand. He puttered around his sister's house for a bit, assessing any maintenance needs that she would never tell him about. After their supper had digested some, he ventured a suggestion."Let's holler at Spence and Paula and see if they want to meet us for some pie downtown."

"You're a bottomless pit," Blair said, rolling her eyes. But she pulled out her phone and sent a text message to Paula.

A moment later, her phone buzzed and, after checking the screen, she looked up at her brother. "It's a go. She said they were just thinking about ice cream, but that Sally's pie sounds even better."

"Great! Are they meeting us there?"

"Yep," Blair answered. Grabbing her keys, she asked, "You riding with me?"

"I'll drive. I'll just head on home from there."

Fifteen minutes later they were all seated at a table and decaf coffee was being poured. Sally made the pies at Sally's Diner, but she wasn't there tonight. She had a vast repertoire, and one never knew what kind of pie would be made on a given day nor how much of it would be left by this time of night.

"So, are we in or out of luck?" Spencer asked the server, whose name tag read 'Stacy.' Just as a confused look was about to form on her pretty face, he clarified, "With regard to pie...what do you have left?"

"Oh," Stacy said, popping her gum discreetly. "Let's see... we have strawberry, a couple of pieces of lemon meringue, one slice of chocolate, and maybe some coconut cream."

As was typical, they ordered one of each. The four of them ate off each other's, getting a taste of every kind. And each variety was delicious. Sally never disappointed. The conversation was light, and for a while, Dexter forgot that Sarah was missing from the scene. Blair and Paula excused themselves to the ladies' room, leaving Dexter and his brother.

When the ticket was delivered, Spencer snatched it up and announced, "I've got it this time." His chair scraped across the floor as he hastily got up to pay at the register. *I don't know what his hurry is,* Dexter thought, *I wasn't going to fight him for it or anything.* A moment later, he heard a woman's laughter, and turned to witness Stacy with her head thrown back in delight at something his big brother had said. *Ah,* that *explains his hurry.* Spencer had to get a little flirting in while his better half was in the bathroom. Dexter just shook his head.

He took a final sip of his coffee and stood up. Scooting up his chair, he turned to face the register. Stacy was twirling her hair and smacking her gum, obviously ensnared by Spencer's charms. Dexter was going to enjoy shattering that. Approaching the brazen pair, Dexter clapped his brother's shoulder. "Is your wife out of the bathroom yet?" he asked. Ignoring the stricken look on Spencer's face, he glanced in Stacy's direction. "What takes women so long in the bathroom anyway?"

"A woman can't tell *all* her secrets," she answered sweetly. She gave him an appraising look. "One of them *your* wife, hon?"

Dexter's sister and sister-in-law spared him from having to answer. When they appeared, he turned to them. "Are we ready?"

There was a murmur in the affirmative and a mild glare from his big brother. Out the door, the four of them dispersed in three separate directions.

Chapter Four

A few weeks passed with no real movement on the divorce. At one point, Dexter wondered if Sarah might be having second thoughts. On impulse, he tried to call her but it went directly to voicemail. He did not leave a message. There was no return call or acknowledgement of his attempt at contact.

After a couple more days had passed, Dexter placed a call to his attorney to assess the status of things. After speaking with him, he didn't know much more than before. Mr. Holland confirmed what Sarah had told Dexter. "As far as I can tell," he said, "she isn't asking for any property except a few pieces of furniture and her car."

"Not that I'm rushing things, but is there something I'm supposed to be doing to keep the ball rolling?"

"The ball's in her court," he replied. "We're just waiting for an official document indicating the terms they're proposing. Our office hasn't heard from her or her counsel in the past..." Dexter could hear papers shuffle as his attorney checked his records. "Oh... thirty days or more," Mr. Holland finished.

"I haven't heard anything from her either," Dexter offered, "but that isn't unusual."

"I can put in a call to her attorney and see if we can get things moving."

"That isn't necessary," Dexter said with a sigh. "I'm not in that big a hurry to be single; it'll happen soon enough."

"Okay then, I'll be in touch when there's news."

Dexter stated his appreciation and ended the call. He stared at the screen of his phone. He couldn't help but worry a little, thinking it seemed odd for Sarah to pull back from the divorce proceedings. He contemplated checking with her parents to see if they'd heard anything from her, but that was likely to backfire. He didn't want to worry them unnecessarily. Finally, a good while later, he opted to send a brief text message. **Hey, hadn't heard from you in a while. Hope everything is ok.**

It showed that the message sent, but not that it had been read. There was no response. While he pondered what could be going on with her, however, he received a text message from Paula. Her neighbor, Christina, had a leak and needed someone to look at a pipe. Of course he'd be happy to assist his good buddy Tony's widow, and told his sister-in-law as much. He checked to see if he had Christina's number stored in his phone and found that he actually did. His next message was to her. She responded promptly, and within fifteen minutes, they had a plan in place for him to drop by the next day to check out the issue that had caused the leak.

It was approaching lunchtime the next day when Dexter checked in with her. Before he could second-guess himself, he instructed her not to eat lunch. He ran by the new place in town and grabbed a couple of sandwiches. He'd been hearing good things about Beth's Bistro. It sounded like Beth was giving Sally a run for her money! Once he'd perused the menu, he understood that Beth's Bistro carried a lighter fare than Sally's Diner. Hopefully, there was enough business in town for both. When he wanted burgers, fries, and pie, Dexter hoped Sally's would be there. But he was thrilled to have a new place that offered things like the chicken salad sandwiches he got for Christina and himself, as well as wraps, soups, and light desserts.

When Dexter arrived, he and Christina enjoyed their sandwiches with some of her terrific lemonade. Beyond that, there was pie (he sure did love some pie!) and good conversation. It felt good to be able to talk about Anthony with someone who also missed him. Oddly, it felt comfortable to talk about Sarah and their impending divorce too. He found himself sharing more with Christina about the situation than he had with anyone. She was very understanding and not judgmental at all. The plumbing situation didn't amount to much. He had it fixed in a jiffy, and arranged for brand new ceiling tiles to replace the ones that now bore water stains. Spencer had some left over from a project, and it was right next door. Dexter wished he could do more. And he had enjoyed the visit so much that he was reluctant to end it.

Christina actually offered to pay him for helping out with the pipe! As if he'd take money for helping out his friend's widow. He made sure she knew to call on him if there was anything else that he could do. He meant it when he offered. In the months since Anthony's death, he had felt so helpless. Dexter knew Christina's sons could tend to her yard and do things around the house, but he hoped that she knew she could call on him to help with things too.

Dexter texted her a few days later to follow up and make sure the pipes were holding up okay. They were. He reminded her to let him know if there was anything else he could do. She seemed grateful, but he doubted he'd hear from her.

Meanwhile, he hadn't heard from Sarah either. It had been *weeks*. Dexter didn't really *want* to talk to her, but he wanted to know everything was okay. He dialed her number. It rang this time, but went to voicemail without her picking up. He left a message this time. "Sarah, it's Dex. Give me a call when you get a chance." He stared at the phone thoughtfully. Who could he call that might know what's going on with her, but wouldn't go off the deep end with worry? Maybe one of Sarah's friends...

But he never made the call. Dexter's phone buzzed with an incoming call from Sarah just then. "Sarah," he answered the call, "Hey, how are you?"

"I'm fine," she said impatiently. "What did you need?"

"Well, I really don't need anything..." he began.

She cut him off. "Then why did you call?" she demanded.

Man, Sarah could press his buttons! She didn't have the time of day for him. He'd been worried about her five minutes ago, but clearly she didn't care if he was dead or alive. Dexter took a deep breath, gathering his patience to deal with her. "Sarah, I haven't talked to you in weeks. You were ready to divorce me, but then my attorney hasn't received anything from yours and nobody's heard anything out of you. You don't answer my texts or call. I was afraid something had happened to you."

"Oh good grief," she said, not bothering to hide her exasperation. Dexter didn't say anything, but she heard him blow out a sigh. "Not that it's any of your business, but I've been out of town."

Sarah's work rarely required her to be out of town. Before he could censor his response, Dexter heard himself saying, "Where? For what?"

"Again," she bit out, "What I do and where I go is none of your business!"

Dexter leaned against the door facing. *God, help me.* "You're right," he conceded. "It's none of my business. I was just concerned."

"You don't need to worry about me. Your lawyer will hear from mine."

"Take care, Sarah," he said, a final attempt at civility.

"I will," she said, and then softened marginally and added, "You too."

Wow, he thought when he hung up, *where did we go wrong?* How did they end up with such bitterness between them? He bowed his head, initially in frustration, but eventually in prayer.

Lord, please make my heart right. Convict me if I'm doing something wrong here, something to provoke Sarah's anger. I'm not even sure it's Your will for us to stay together, so I won't pray for that. I just pray that Your will be done. And if it be Your will, Father, I pray that this anger in Sarah's heart will fade with time. Help us to at least be civil to one another.

And Lord, be with the Sinclairs.

And keep Spencer in line.

Amen.

~~~~~~~~~

Summer proceeded and was largely uneventful. The *end* of summer, however, was rather eventful indeed. Labor Day weekend, specifically, was a humdinger of a time. His divorce from Sarah was finally complete on that Friday. On Saturday, he attended a cookout at Christina Sinclair's home, as did Spencer and Paula. His dear brother managed to make a horse's hiney out of himself, and to beat it all, it was with Christina. He had the audacity to come on to Christina! His neighbor! His neighbor who was friends with his wife!

The day after the cookout, Dexter dropped by Spencer and Paula's house after church. They were just finishing up with lunch when he got there.

"Come on in," Paula welcomed. "Would you like a sandwich?"

"Maybe just one to go," Dexter answered, "I need to borrow your husband real quick."

"Oh, okay." She was already smearing mustard on a slice of bread and slapping a sandwich together. "Something wrong?"

"I hope not," he said, willing her not to ask any questions that would force him to lie.

His eyes bore into his older brother. "I just need him to take a look at something." *Like my fist coming at his face!*

"Sure," Spencer said hesitantly, pushing back from the table. "Let me just put my shoes back on."

Dexter took the sandwich from Paula with a mutter of thanks. He took a significant bite out of it while waiting on the front porch for Spencer. When he heard his big brother coming, Dexter bit off another third of the sandwich and hustled down the steps. By the time Spencer joined him in his truck, he was finished eating. Neither of them said a word until Dexter parked his truck at a vacant parking lot.

He put the truck in park, killed the motor, and turned to face Spencer. "Help me understand what happened last night."

"*Nothing* happened."

"Let's try this again," Dexter spat through gritted teeth, "I *know* what happened, but you're my brother, and I want to know what you have to say for yourself."

Spencer was backed into a corner and could think of little to say in his own defense. His nostrils flared as he let out a frustrated breath. Dexter waited wordlessly. "I'll admit things got a little out of hand…" he began.

"Oh, is *that* what you call it?" Dexter interjected. Striking the dash suddenly, he shouted, "You had her trapped, Spencer! She didn't want what you were selling!"

"I'm not so sure about…"

"I *am*. I heard enough to know! Christina is a good, decent woman who has been through enough without some moron putting the moves on her. And besides that, Spence, you *have* a good woman who loves you. Why do you have to act like you do?"

The question hung heavily in the air. The answer was slow in coming, and when it arrived, it didn't satisfy either of them. Spencer released a breath and said, "I don't know."

Dexter waited a beat, shaking his head. "I love you, bro," he said quietly, "but you give our gender a bad rep. You give our family a bad name. And don't forget who you're representing here on earth." He stopped short of quoting 2 Corinthians 5:20.

Spencer looked out the window. He hated being preached to by his little brother, but he knew Dexter was right. And to make matters worse, he had no explanation for his actions. Spencer loved Paula, and the idea of hurting her should be enough to keep him from straying. But somehow he was able to compartmentalize, keeping thoughts of his wife separate when the urge to pursue something new struck.

Dexter allowed a span of silence to stretch out between them, each lost in his own thoughts. Finally, he spoke. "Look, Paula's love should be enough to keep you in check, but if it's not, then at least don't embarrass yourself by going after someone who doesn't want you. And in case you're still not clear on it, Christina Sinclair does *not* want you. And if you ever so much as *look* at her again...," He paused long enough for Spencer to look around at him expectantly. "...You'll have *me* to answer to."

Spencer wanted to say something to take the focus off himself. He wanted to comment about Dexter's sudden interest in his neighbor's honor. But he didn't. Common sense wouldn't let him. He couldn't remember when he'd seen Dexter so riled, and the man knew a lot of dirt on him. So instead, he asked, "Are we finished here?"

"As long as we have an understanding."

Spencer looked out the window. Dexter waited, watching until he nodded his head ever so slightly.

"Good." He started the engine and took his brother home.

On Monday, Labor Day, he tried to do some damage control by having a conversation with Christina. He could only imagine what she must be thinking of their family. She was a dear though, her primary concern being for Paula. She was somewhere between appalled and amused when she realized Dexter had confronted his brother in defense of her honor. She denied making any assumptions about him based on his brother's behavior, and Dexter believed her.

Christina was *so* easy to talk to. Dexter hadn't had a ton of experience with women, and realized he had always assumed that Blair's easygoing disposition was a pleasant fluke -- because Sarah was anything *but* easy going -- especially the past few years. It was like she was just waiting for Dexter to mess up, say something wrong. She was quick to jump to conclusions. In contrast, Christina acted like it hadn't even occurred to her that Dexter might be a heel simply because Spencer had acted like one. This unassuming nature of hers was refreshing. He had found a friend in her. That was evident by the end of the visit, for it was while he was there that both he and Christina experienced unpleasant developments.

Dexter's phone buzzed, a glance at the screen revealing a call from Blair. He excused himself to take the call.

"Hey Sis," he answered.

"Hey Dex, whatcha up to?"

"Cleaning up one of Spencer's messes."

"Oh no," she said, "What'd he do this time?"

"Nothing I care to get into," he replied. "What's up?"

"Have you talked to Sarah?" she asked tentatively.

"Nope."

"I take it the divorce went through…"

"Yes, it was final on Friday."

"Did you know she was seeing someone?"

The question punched him in the gut. He had often wondered, but had never given voice to it. The wound was to his pride more than his heart at this point, but it was a wound nonetheless. He realized he hadn't answered when Blair prompted him. "Dex?"

"I'm here."

"Dex, Sarah remarried on Saturday. Someone from Winchester."

"Wow," he said, struggling to find more words to express what he was feeling.

"Yeah," said Blair, offering, "I'm sorry."

"She didn't waste any time, huh?"

"From what I've heard, they've been travelling all over the place."

How could he tell his sister that he'd rather not know what all she'd heard? None of it mattered and all of it was painful.

"Well, I hope she will be happy. God knows she wasn't happy with me."

"You're a good man, Dex. Too good for her."

"Thanks for saying that, Sis. We've all got good in us -- even Sarah," he chuckled.

"Aw, Dex -- you don't even know you just proved my point."

When he shared the news with Christina, she eased the blow a little more. It was really good to have a friend. She was struggling to find her way without her spouse too. The Sinclairs had been friends with two other couples, and Christina didn't seem to quite fit in anymore. While he was on the phone with Blair, Christina had discovered that their friends had gone on their annual Labor Day excursion without her. It cut her deeply, not so much that they went but that they didn't include her on the decision to go or how to handle the fact that one of them was now missing. Dexter understood. It was difficult to suddenly be adrift in a world of couples.

They had a lot of common ground, he and Christina. He was glad that it worked out that they happened to be together when they both had stuff to process. He found that their losses were similar even though they were different, and they were connected in ways he never would have predicted.

Chapter Five

Dexter waited until the end of the week, but ultimately, he couldn't resist texting Sarah. He felt the need to let her know that he knew about her marriage and that he wished her no ill will.

I understand congratulations are in order. Hope you've found happiness. I wish you the best.

Out of curiosity, he watched to see if it was read after it was delivered. It was, almost immediately. The reply, however, didn't come for an hour or so. A simple **Thanks** was all he got. Did she doubt his sincerity? Did he come across as sarcastic? He reread the message he had sent. He thought it sounded sincere enough. Dexter had done what was on his heart to do. The way Sarah received it was not his responsibility. He could only do his part. Maybe Sarah would let her guard down eventually and realize he wasn't the enemy.

It took a couple of weeks, but the idea that Sarah had been seeing her new husband before she had left him finally dawned on Dexter. He thought back to the way things suddenly went downhill, how she found fault with everything he did or said. At the time, he had foolishly thought it was a phase or a hormonal issue. He had bent over backward to try and get along with her, but he realized now that Sarah had checked out of their marriage long before she had even left. Not only had she fallen out of love with him, but chances are, Sarah had fallen *in* love with someone else. With a new love in her life, there was no motivation to nurture her marriage to Dexter.

This revelation prompted a whole new level of reflection. What had he done wrong? How could he have prevented the demise of his marriage? Had Sarah fallen in love with someone else because she was no longer in love with him or had she fallen out of love with him because someone else had captured her heart? Regardless of which came first, how could it have been avoided? Had he not invested in his marriage? Had he taken her for granted?

Dexter had adjusted to living alone, but still felt a void. There was a longing in his heart for someone with whom to share his life. But the thought of giving his heart to someone new was terrifying when there were so many unanswered questions. He didn't know if he'd ever be able to move on. Perhaps another visit with Brother James was warranted.

That opportunity came about mid-October, and Dexter didn't even have to initiate it. He shook Brother James' hand as he was leaving church on Sunday, and before he could say anything, the pastor said, "How are things going? Want to get together this week?" When Dexter marvelled that he was just about to schedule a time to meet, Pastor James just chuckled and said, "That usually means God is involved. He gave us both the same nudge at the same time."

They met at Sally's this time and chatted over coffee. When Brother James inquired as to how things were going, Dexter didn't beat around the bush. "I guess you've heard that Sarah has remarried."

"I had thought perhaps it was only a rumor," the older man replied.

"It's true. She married the day after the divorce was final," Dexter revealed without a trace of bitterness, though in all honesty, he had to work to keep it out of his voice.

Pastor James leaned back in his chair. "And how do you feel about that?"

"Well," Dexter said, "I've been through a whole range of emotions with it." He paused and then continued when the pastor nodded.. "I've prayed so much about our marriage and really didn't want to let go. But I think Sarah gave up on us a long time ago. I truly hope she is happy."

"What about you? Are *you* happy?"

"I'm okay."

"But not happy."

"Well… I'm not *un*happy."

The pastor had a way of urging him to talk without saying a word. He just waited. And Dexter filled the silence. "I don't know," he said, "I'm fine. I just can't seem to find that contentment that Blair has with being single. But I can't think about being in another relationship without knowing why my marriage ended like it did."

"You're afraid," Pastor James observes.

"Maybe," Dexter admitted. "I guess I'm not excited about putting my heart out there after this fiasco. But more than that, I just don't want to fail again. That's what divorce feels like -- failure." The pastor nodded his understanding. He took a long sip of his coffee, and then he spoke.

"Let me ask you something, Dex… has God convicted your heart of any particular shortcoming in regard to your marriage?"

Dex thought about it for a moment before answering. "Not really," he said, "Only in hindsight, I know I may have become too comfortable. I assumed that she was committed like I was."

"But she wasn't -- and that isn't your fault. We've talked about this; you're only accountable for your own actions."

"I know. But you understand, right? Being leery of trying again?"

"That's because it isn't time yet." Dexter didn't say anything, only studied the older man across the table. Pastor James went on. "Everything you've expressed is a natural part of healing. God will use this to prepare your heart for whatever comes next. And when He moves you and when He has placed the right person in your life, then *not* going for it will become scarier than *going* for it."

Dexter grinned. He wanted to believe his pastor. And he knew the Lord would work in that way. He just had to be patient and put it in God's hands. "I'm overthinking it, huh?" he said.

"You don't have to figure it all out; just trust the One who already *has* it figured out."

Just give it to God, Dexter thought. Again, he felt like a burden had been lifted. What a relief to remember that God is in control!

~~~~~~~~~~~

Over the course of the next few weeks, Dexter let that reminder sink in. He knew Pastor James was right because he had seen God work that way in his life before. He knew that God had the big picture and that He had His hand on every aspect of his life. So he relaxed and stayed busy with work as the holidays approached.

Dexter's family and buddies had started to tease him about entering the dating scene. This was something he and Christina commiserated about -- people not letting them proceed at their own pace. Of course, Dexter had had a little more time to adjust to being single. He could understand even more why Christina would not be ready to consider dating. Plus the fact that Anthony had died -- and died suddenly. At least Dexter had lost his spouse in degrees over time.

Still, Christina was young and had so much to offer. And she was beautiful. And *so* easy to talk to. Dexter felt like he'd known her all his life. In truth, he *had* known her for years. But their current situation had allowed them to nurture a friendship that might otherwise have seemed inappropriate. He was enjoying their friendship immensely. In many ways, she had been a Godsend. She understood the issues that came with being newly alone as she was wading through them herself.

Dexter dropped by to see Christina before heading next door to his brother's home for Thanksgiving dinner. It was a spur of the moment decision, but he was so glad he did. Good-natured banter and the warmth of a buzzing kitchen and loving home stirred something in him. His own home, now silent and empty, had never had a vibe like Christina's. The Sinclair children were wonderful, and he found himself wondering what it would have been like if he and Sarah had started a family all those years ago. Would it have bound them together? Or would their divorce have been inevitable and only complicated by custody issues?

He knew there was no point in playing the "what if?" game. Wondering what might have been was only a torturous and non-productive way to pass the time. Dexter cherished his niece and nephew, Spencer's children, though they were now grown and had moved away. He would just focus on his extended family. And his blessings. Sure, life had taken a different turn than he would have chosen. But Dexter knew he was a blessed man. It *was* the season of giving thanks after all. And he *was* thankful for all his blessings. Among those blessings was his friendship with Christina Sinclair and her family.

Sarah had been gone for a while now, and Dexter had been through all the firsts without her -- their anniversary, Christmas, birthdays, etc. When she left, she knew it was for good and she cut all ties. Dexter had leaned heavily on family in her absence. Christina was only just now facing each first without Tony. She had her children, which was a comfort, but didn't seem to have the extended family support that Dexter did. And he wasn't sure what was up with her close friends, but he knew that Christina was struggling with every new obstacle she faced.

He didn't hear much out of her through Christmas, but understood that she and her family had sought out an alternative way to get through the holidays. Dexter was delighted to learn, however, that they would be joining the New Year's Eve celebration at Spencer and Paula's.

It was there that a brilliant idea was born. The next uncomfortable holiday coming up was Valentine's Day. A holiday set aside for couples was miserable for people in his situation, and of course, Christina's. Dexter, in particular, dreaded all the questions about Valentine's Day plans and the pity he would receive from people when he admitted to having none. Christina was in a similar predicament. Two friends, both alone on a day set aside for lovers. They weren't lovers, of course, but why not ease the loneliness of the dreaded day by planning to spend it together? Christina was reluctant, but ultimately agreed with his logic.

Then came the surprising thing. Dexter began to look forward to their plans, began to think about Christina fondly, and began to recognize the reality of their circumstances. Tony had been a good friend to him and a loving husband to Christina… but he was gone and would never be back. And with Sarah remarried, it was clear that she was not going to be back either. Both Dexter and Christina were untethered. Single. Available. And as far as Dexter could tell, they were compatible. They had common interests -- if nothing else, they had both loved Anthony -- and were both believers. He realized he was starting to see her differently, starting to wonder if there could ever be something more between them. At first it seemed wrong to notice Christina's beauty, to miss her when they weren't together, to admit that a conversation with her could brighten his day. But then he acknowledged that his feelings for her were rooted in friendship, but growing steadily. And maybe that was okay.

During the cold first month of the year, Dexter began to pray specifically about his friendship with Christina. He didn't want to jeopardize their friendship, but found that he was more open than he would have ever imagined to the possibility of pursuing more than a friendly relationship with her. *Would she ever be open to it?* He wondered. In time, of course… Dexter knew he couldn't rush her or scare her away or make their friendship awkward. He didn't know how to proceed. He only knew that he felt a glimmer of chance, a subtle… *nudge*. Recalling what Pastor James had said, he could only hope that God was in this. And so he prayed…

Dear Lord, have You *planted this feeling in my heart? Are You trying to show me that there's something more there? I never thought I'd feel ready to love again, and certainly not so soon. But I care for Christina very much. If it is Your will, Father, I pray that You will present the opportunity for us to explore a different level of our relationship. I don't have much to offer, Lord, and it's awfully easy for me to believe Christina wouldn't be interested -- Sarah wasn't, after all. But I know that if this has Your blessing, You'll be whispering to her too. Help me to be patient, Lord, because I know she's at a different place in her healing. Whether it's me or not, I pray that You will bring someone into her life that will be a comfort, someone who will love her and bring happiness into her life.* Dexter's heart whispered, "Let it be me," though he did not form the words as he closed out his prayer.

All he could do was wait, and hope Christina wouldn't change her mind about Valentine's Day.

Chapter Six

As Valentine's Day approached, Dexter's thoughts turned more and more toward the possibility of a romantic relationship with Christina. He couldn't believe that he was actually ready to consider it, but once the idea formed in his mind and heart, he couldn't seem to shake it. Through their many conversations and on top of a solid foundation of friendship, Dexter found that he was not only open to exploring more than a friendship with Christina, but truthfully, he was already falling for her. He was apprehensive though. What if she didn't feel the same way? What if he ruined their friendship with the suggestion? Dexter did a lot of praying in the week before their "non-date." His prayer was that, if God was in this, that He would pave the way. He prayed that God would give him a peace about it and provide an opportunity to bring it up with Christina. He also prayed that God would speak to Christina's heart.

The day before Valentine's Day, Dexter was surprisingly calm. He had arranged for Christina to come over and just hang out. He planned to cook for her and keep things low key. Rather than going out in the world of couples, Christina was receptive to staying in and watching a movie or something.

When she arrived, she positively took his breath away. Yes, he was definitely smitten. But he played it cool, ushering her in and making her a cup of tea. It was a cold day, and some tea and warm conversation hit the spot. When Christina's stomach growled, they started supper. The pair worked side by side in Dexter's kitchen, making it easy for him to imagine evenings spent as a couple.

It was during the meal that a window of opportunity presented itself. Christina made the remark that it was a good thing this wasn't a *real* date. Dexter's stomach dropped. "Why?" he asked with trepidation.

"Because there's no way to eat spaghetti gracefully," she replied lightly.

Relief flooded through him and, before he could stop himself, he said, "When we start dating, I'll be sure to make something else." This gave her pause, but Dexter explained that he would not push her or make things awkward. He would wait until she was ready, but that when the time was right and if she was so inclined, he would be very interested in courting her.

She didn't say no. Dexter knew she had some healing yet to do though. He kept his word, keeping the evening light and easy between them. There was no awkwardness as they finished their dinner and watched their movie. Dexter and Christina successfully got through Valentine's Day.

Anthony had been gone almost a year, and Christina knew Dexter's intentions. Now he just had to be patient and grateful for their friendship. Christina was very passionate about some mission work she was doing in Anthony's memory. Dexter was supportive as she presented at various churches, speaking of the rewarding nature of the work and eliciting volunteers and monetary support for their endeavors. The entire Sinclair family was involved. Dexter longed to get involved too, primarily because it was good work and God was tugging on his heart, but also, he had to admit, because he wanted to work alongside Christina and her family.

The cold days of winter passed, fading into a memory in the presence of a lovely spring. The zeal Christina had for her mission endeavors was contagious. Dexter accompanied Christina on a day trip to the children's hospital in April, enjoying the commute almost as much as witnessing Christina with those babies. Following her lead, Dexter jumped in and began reading Easter stories to the youngsters who were tethered to oxygen tanks and IV poles. Their presence allowed for parents to take a much-needed break for a shower or a nap or a meal with family.

By the end of the day, Dexter knew that he was all in. He wanted to be a part of every aspect of this mission endeavor, and the fact that this meant working with Christina was now just a fringe benefit. In speaking with her and her family about how gratifying the work was, Dexter came to realize that Christina carried a lot of guilt about not following Anthony's prompts through the years. If she had gotten involved before, she wouldn't have "robbed him of the blessings." There were times when Christina acknowledged that Anthony's seed was planted and that she was cultivating it, but at other times, she still struggled with the guilt.

It was Dexter who finally put her mind at ease once and for all. "I knew Tony pretty well," he said. "I never knew him to sit idly on something the Lord was asking him to do. I can't help but believe that if it had been on his heart to move forward with it, no force would've stopped him from trying... and certainly not just a lukewarm response from his family. He wasn't that easily deterred."

"He *wasn't* easily deterred," Christina agreed. "Especially if he thought God was asking something of him."

"Christina, I believe that Anthony did what God laid on his heart to do -- he planted the seed that would be cultivated at the right time. And you're doing that work now -- just like God is asking you to. The way I see it, you have nothing to feel guilty about. If you guys had jumped in back when he mentioned it, the whole thing might have taken a different turn. Think of all those little ones, the families whose lives you've touched -- their particular needs didn't even exist at that point. God knew their needs ahead of time and was setting things in motion to address them before they even existed!" He gave her a moment to digest what he was saying and then went on. "Christina, you did exactly what needed to be done exactly *when* it needed to be done. No guilt."

A slow smile spread across her face, radiating into her eyes as she owned this truth. "Thank you, Dexter," she said. "That actually makes a lot of sense."

He could read the relief and gratitude in her eyes and believed that he had gotten through to her. Life was too short to carry unnecessary guilt. Christina was a warm, caring person with a heart of gold. He couldn't bear the thought of her feeling badly over not starting such amazing mission work sooner. All any of us can do is move forward from the present anyway, but he truly believed that she was doing the right thing at the right time.

Plans were underway for a coordinated effort throughout the summer. Christina had mission teams going every weekend to tend to the needs of sick children and their families. She had a designated contact person at every church she'd addressed; that person signed on new volunteers and accepted donations of money, gift cards, earbuds, phone chargers, toys, books, Bibles, etc. The Anthony Sinclair Missionary Foundation was a huge success, and Dexter couldn't be prouder of Christina.

Meanwhile, it had been several weeks since Dexter had intimated the fact that he hoped for more than friendship from Christina. He had prayed for patience as she continued to process her grief and until her heart was ready to consider romantic love again. They had fallen right back into their roles as friends without missing a beat. No awkward moments, no flirting, no disagreements about how to proceed. They were friends and, Dexter thought, that might be all they'd ever be -- though he was certain Christina would always carry a piece of his heart. Once Haley was back home from college for the summer, he didn't talk to Christina as much. He missed her, but knew that Haley and the others deserved to have the lion's share of her attention.

Dexter was thrilled to hear from Christina the last week of May. She extended an invitation to a Memorial Day cookout at her home. On the telephone, she told Dexter that Haley had a new friend that she wanted everyone to meet. A *male* friend who might be getting involved with the mission work.

"Sounds good," he said, "What can I bring?"

"Hmm," Christina said, pretending to think. "I seem to recall that you're good with spaghetti. How are you with other kinds of pasta? Maybe a pasta salad?"

"I can do that," he agreed.

"Spencer and Paula will be here, I think. Will you invite Blair?" Christina had only met his sister briefly, but seemed eager to get to know her better.

"Sure," he replied.

"Great!" she said, "I'm looking forward to it. I think Becca and Gail might even come this time."

"Um... Christina?"

"Yes?"

"What kind of noodles should I use in the pasta salad?"

Odd question, she thought... and then she recalled their conversation. "What are you asking, Dex?"

He could hear her smiling, and was encouraged. "I'm asking if you have a preference in noodles." Dexter held his breath, waiting to see how she would respond.

"It doesn't matter," she said casually, adding, "as long as it's something I can eat gracefully."

Realization dawned swiftly and Dexter stifled himself before letting out a whoop. He pumped a fist in the air exuberantly.

"Dex?"

"Yeah, I'm here. I can totally do that," he said. "I'm your man!" *In more ways than one*, he thought.

And on the other end of the line, Christina thought *I could get used to hearing that.*

~~~~~~~~~~

Dexter tried not to read too much into it. She *could* have just been talking about noodles, after all. But he was cautiously optimistic. And regardless of whether Christina meant what he thought (hoped) she did, he was looking forward to seeing her. He enjoyed being around Christina's family and was excited about the cookout.

He hoped, for her sake, that her friends, Becca and Gail, would be there. Christina had had a particularly tough time with finding her fit with the couples with whom she and Anthony had spent time. Dexter knew that these couples had endured a loss with Tony's death too, but in some ways it seemed like they'd alienated Christina when she needed them most. Everyone dealt with loss in their own way, he supposed. Maybe they were finding resolution now, he thought. The cookout would be a good thing.

Remembering Christina's request that he invite Blair, he shot his sister a text message.

Hey, sis -- wanna go to a cookout on Memorial Day?

Her reply came right away. **Sure. Where?**

You remember my friend Christina that lives next to Spence. She wants us all to come.

Awesome. Should I bring something? Blair was on board.

I'm supposed to bring pasta salad. That's all I know.

Laughing, Blair tapped out, **I'll make a dessert or something. Lmk what time.**

Dexter agreed, and then spent the evening perusing recipes for pasta salads online. There were hundreds! Who knew? None of them called for spaghetti noodles though, he noted with a grin. He had tried to be patient, but he was hoping to move out of the friend zone soon.

The day of the cookout found Christina busy with preparations. She was quickly growing fond of Haley's boyfriend, Jared. After spending a couple of weeks with his own family, he had joined Haley for the long weekend. When Christina put her children to work getting ready for the cookout, he didn't have to be asked. She could see him out the window scouring off the patio. She remarked to Haley, who was helping her clean the kitchen, that he certainly seemed to be a great guy.

"Right?" she answered with a smile. "I can't wait for him to meet everyone else. Thanks for having the cookout, Mom."

Christina gave her a brief side-hug as she reached for her ringing phone. It was Dexter.

"Hello?" she answered.

"I have two different kinds of pasta salad made, and wondered if you need me to do anything else."

"Wow! That's fantastic! Why two? You didn't have to do that."

"You didn't tell me what kind, and there are so many kinds. I made one with radiatore pasta, peas, crab, and ranch dressing. The other has shells, cherry tomatoes, bacon, cucumbers, and mayo. I can bring them on over and help you with whatever you're doing."

Christina laughed. "I never refuse good help," she said.

"Okay then, do you need anything? I can pick up whatever you need me to."

"Do you have a cooler?"

"Yes, ma'am," he answered, hoping Sarah hadn't taken it.

"Bring it if you don't mind, and stop to get a couple of bags of ice. I have one cooler, but I thought I might set out two -- one for soft drinks and one for bottles of water."

"Okay, sounds good. Wait -- you're not having lemonade?"

"Yes, of course," she answered, chuckling at the pout in his voice. "I made it just for you."

"Awesome!" he said, "Don't I feel special?!"

"You *are* special," she replied lightly.

Dexter chuckled and told Christina he'd see her in an hour or so. Was she flirting a little? That definitely sounded a little flirty. *Didn't it?* He talked himself in and out of believing Christina was being mildly flirtatious, but regardless of his conclusion, Dexter couldn't wipe the smile off his face. It was still there when he arrived forty-three minutes later, ice and pasta in tow.

He went around to the patio, emptying ice into the coolers. It was there that he encountered Jared. Wiping his wet hands on his pants, he extended his right one. "Dexter Billings," he said.

"Jared. Jared Hughes. Nice to meet you."

"I'm a friend of the family. My brother lives next door," Dexter explained.

"Yes, Haley had mentioned you. I'm her boyfriend."

"She's a great young lady."

"She is," Jared agreed. "I'm a lucky guy."

Just then, the back door opened. "Dexter!" Christina said, "You're here!" He answered her with a broad grin. She looked radiant. She wore the season so well, with a red sleeveless blouse and denim capris, her hair pulled back in a clip. He realized he hadn't said anything when she went on, "I see you've met Jared."

"Yes, we were just talking," Dexter said. His mouth seemed to have gone dry suddenly.

Haley stepped out the door silently behind her mother. She and Jared exchanged a knowing look, though

Dexter couldn't read exactly what it was about. "Haley," Dexter said warmly, "it's so good to see you."

"You too," she replied with a smile.

"I bet you're glad to be home for the summer."

"I am," Haley agreed. They chatted about summer plans while they put beverages into the coolers.

Dexter fetched the pasta salad from his vehicle and then worked happily alongside Christina in the kitchen. Haley and Jared were in and out, working mostly outside. Payton and his girlfriend, Lily, showed up, pitching in to carry chairs and do whatever Christina bade them do. Soon enough, Jordan and Brianna, Spencer and Paula, Blair, and other guests began to arrive.

Like Christina, Dexter drifted in and out of conversations and enjoyed the company of many guests. Christina, he knew, was careful to avoid being alone with Spencer. Nobody wanted a repeat of the previous cookout, which was nearly disastrous because of Spencer's antics. Dexter kept a close eye on his brother though, and he seemed to be walking the straight and narrow. *Good*, he thought. Maybe his little chat had worked.

Brent, Gail, Justin, and Becca -- Christina's longtime friends -- arrived together and stayed for about an hour and a half. He would have never said so to Christina, but their attendance appeared obligatory. He was glad they came though, and Christina seemed positively thrilled.

Dexter enjoyed the evening, enjoyed seeing Christina in action. He resisted the urge to follow her around and look for opportunities to talk. His patience was rewarded about 9:00 when most of the crowd had dispersed. Those who remained were Christina's children and their respective paramours. Paula had left reluctantly. Only after helping sack up the trash and being reassured that the Sinclairs could get the rest of the cleanup did she join Spencer in the trek across yards to their home. At that point, Haley and Brianna shooed Christina and Dexter away as they finished up in the kitchen.

Christina hesitated only briefly before offering the girls a grateful smile and then turning to Dexter. "Want to do some porch-sitting?"

"Sure," he said, "I'm going to top off my lemonade, and I'll meet you there."

"I'll take one too," she said easily.

When Dexter came out to the porch, Christina was seated in the swing. For a moment, he was uncertain where to sit. In his mind, he debated the suggestion of intimacy that might come with sitting next to her on the swing versus the aloofness that she might assume if he stood casually near the porch railing. Or he could sit on the chair a few feet away, but that would be far less conducive to the private conversation he hoped they'd be having. His mind raced with the different scenarios, all that in the span of time it took him to walk across the porch. He almost broke a sweat with his internal debate, only to find Christina sweetly patting the swing next to her with one hand as she took her lemonade from him with the other. He should've known to just take his cues from her. He should've realized that this amazing woman would make things easy.

Dexter sat down carefully on the swing next to her. For a moment they said nothing as they found their rhythm, swinging gently in amicable silence. He was acutely aware of her warm, sun-kissed shoulders next to him. He tried not to acknowledge her denim-clad thighs as they brushed his. There was definitely an intimacy to sharing a swing. The silence was comfortable, but Dexter was longing to know what was on Christina's mind. He was dying to know where he stood.

"The cookout turned out great," he commented.

"Yeah, I think everyone had a good time," she replied.

There was a quiet moment. A cricket chirped from within the hydrangea bush, its song echoed by the soft rhythm of the creaking chain that held their weight. Dexter took a long sip of his lemonade. Christina asked, "What did you think of Haley's young man?"

"I'm very impressed," Dexter said honestly. "He seems like a terrific guy."

"I believe he is. I'm so glad they found each other."

"They act like they've known one another for ages. Have they been seeing each other long?"

"Actually," Christina said, "They *have*."

"Really? I don't remember you talking about him."

"That's the funny thing," Christina revealed carefully, "...I didn't know."

"Wait..." Dexter said, obviously puzzled, "Haley talks to you about everything. What do you mean you didn't know?"

"She was being considerate," Christina explained. "She met Jared before her daddy died, but hadn't had a chance to tell us about him. Then she said that she couldn't bear to 'flaunt a new relationship' when I had just lost my companion."

"Wow," Dexter said, taking it in. "That's very thoughtful." He paused, and then turned to look at

Christina. "That's been way over a year though. I can't believe she didn't mention him this whole time."

"I know. Her heart was in the right place, but I told her I wished I'd known. Jared was there for her through her grief and everything. It would have been a comfort to know she had someone."

"You have a remarkable daughter," he offered.

"Yes," Christina agreed, adding, "and I believe God placed a remarkable young man in her life at just the right time."

Dexter nodded his agreement. He pushed them softly with his feet, mulling over this development. He couldn't believe Haley and Jared had been dating this entire time! And out of consideration for her mother, hadn't said anything. She had waited... for what? Suddenly he stopped pushing the swing.

"What's wrong?" Christina asked.

"What made Haley decide to tell you *now*?"

"Well, I guess she thought it was time." The swing began to sway once more. Christina continued, "I mean....like you said, it's been more than a year." She felt the swing pick up just a little momentum. "Plus, Jared is pretty eager to get involved with the mission work," she added. Christina could *feel* rather than see Dexter nodding next to her. She ventured on, glad that he couldn't see her face in the darkness. "And it could've had a little something to do with what *I* shared with *her*."

The swing ceased its swaying motion again as Dexter's curiosity piqued. "What did you share with her?" he asked quietly, sensing the importance of what she was about to impart.

Christina was suddenly very nervous. What if he'd changed his mind by now? *He told you he'd wait.* She took a deep breath and glanced in his direction. She couldn't quite look him in the eye though. She picked at an imaginary speck on her pants, gathering courage to address the question. "Well...you know...I just mentioned," she stammered, "I was telling her about the conversation you and I had in February." Christina didn't dare to look at him. She scraped furiously at the offending speck on her pants.

Dexter found it positively endearing that Christina was so unsettled. He resisted the urge to tease her and make it worse. "You told her that I wanted more than friendship," he stated. Without waiting for confirmation, he asked, "And what did she say?"

"She's fine with it," Christina said. Finally finding her courage to face him, she looked in his direction. In the dimness of the evening, she smiled. "She was fine, too, when I told her I thought I might be ready for more as well."

The swing stopped more abruptly than ever this time, as Dexter pivoted in his seat to look into Christina's eyes. "Are you serious?!"

"If you're still interested..."

"Of course, I'm still interested! I'd be a fool not to be. Are you sure? I've tried not to rush you..."

"You've been very patient. I haven't felt rushed at all," she said. She cast him a reassuring smile. "I'm sure the reservations I have are the same things you've thought about. I treasure our friendship and don't want to ruin it." Dexter waited, only nodding to confirm that he shared that concern. He truly felt that God had nudged him toward her though. Would she understand that? Christina answered that question without him giving voice to it. "I've prayed about it a lot, and feel that the circumstances and the timing are more than coincidence. I feel that maybe we're supposed to give this a chance. Does that make sense?"

"It more than makes sense," he replied with a ebullient grin. He stopped short of trying to explain that he had prayed similarly, received the same peace about it, and felt certain God was bringing them together. He suddenly felt very confident that there would be time to share all of that with her later… *after* he had won her heart.

Chapter Seven

Dexter was on cloud nine when he returned home that evening. He combed over his time with Christina, revisiting each bit of their conversation and recalling the cadence of her laughter. She was so beautiful and unassuming. The memory of their conversation warmed his heart and brought a smile to his face. Dexter accentuated their discussion by offering his hand, palm up, which Christina took. Their first venture into this new territory was ushered in with laced fingers and the gentle swaying of the porch swing. It felt, oddly, both bold and natural. It was as if her hand belonged in his, and yet, it was so exhilarating that the memory of it took his breath.

He should be tired. It was late, and he had spent a lot of nervous energy in anticipation of the evening. Dexter got ready for bed and spent some time thanking God for His guidance. He could not, however, stay focused. Nor could he sleep. And he couldn't seem to wipe that silly smile off his face. Dexter wondered if Christina was in such a state. Probably not, he decided. Could he get so lucky as to have her already that smitten with him?

On impulse, Dexter picked up his phone to text her and say good night. To his delight, he found a text message from her waiting for him.

Thank you for all your help today and for a great evening.

The message had come through twenty minutes prior, so he had no idea if Christina was still up. He tapped out a reply, regardless.

It doesn't get much better than the evening we had. Thank YOU. GN, Christina.

He watched as the message went through. His iPhone reported it to be delivered. He watched. Was she still up? And then his screen showed that the message was read. He smiled, feeling sixteen. A few seconds later, her simple reply came.

GN, Dexter. It was punctuated with a smiley face, which evoked the memory of her smile. He sighed. He never expected to feel this way again. *Again?* Had he ever felt this way before? Dexter's early courtship with Sarah was such a distant memory now that he could hardly compare the two, and knew he probably shouldn't anyway. All he knew was that he felt contentment in his heart and hope for his future... and a flutter in his stomach at the very thought of Christina Sinclair.

~~~~~~~~~~

Dexter's week was full, as always seemed to be the case after a holiday weekend. Regrettably, he didn't have a lot of time to pursue Christina. On the bright side, however, thoughts of her filled his mind and passed the time while he worked. He made it a point to greet her each morning by text message, and they spoke on the phone a couple of times that week.

He tried to be sensitive to the possibility that Christina might want to ease into being a public pair, but he was itching to officially take her out now that she had given him the go-ahead. He thought that maybe dinner and a movie in a neighboring town was an acceptable solution. He proposed the idea during a mid-week phone conversation with Christina.

"Are you busy Saturday night?" he asked.

"I'm meeting with the Director of Missions at four, but that shouldn't take long."

"I wondered if you'd like to go over to Green Hollow for some dinner? We could see the new Kendrick Brothers movie."

"That sounds perfect," she responded, meaning it. She loved the idea of going out of town to wet her feet in this new pool, though she would have never articulated it nor held out for it. It was almost as if Dexter had read her mind. "I should be done by five," she offered.

Dexter agreed to pick her up around 5:30. Now, all he had to do was get through the rest of the week.

~~~~~~~~~~

He was thankful for a full work week. When Saturday came and he finally had some down time, Dexter was a veritable bundle of nerves. He spent some time that morning with a mug of hot coffee and his favorite book of devotions. After that, he put it in God's hands and turned his attention to sprucing up his SUV.

With a clean ride and an afternoon to kill, Dexter texted his sister to see what she was up to. Blair, in response, asked if he'd be interested in grabbing some lunch.

Sure, something light though. Eating out later.

Meet you at Beth's in 30? Blair suggested.

Dexter agreed. When he arrived, Blair already had a table and was waiting for him. "I ordered a lemonade for you," she said as he sat down.

"Thanks." He picked up a menu and looked over it. "What are you having?"

"I think I'm going for a panini," she said, studying her own menu and then laying it aside. Dexter took a sip of his lemonade and winced. Blair noticed. "What's wrong? Isn't it any good?"

"It's okay," he replied, "but it pales in comparison to Christina's."

"She *does* make good lemonade," Blair agreed.

When the server returned, Dexter ordered a club sandwich, then directed his attention back to his sister. "So, did you enjoy the cookout?"

"Yeah, that was fun. They all seem really nice."

Dexter nodded his head, not trusting himself to say more. Subsequent conversation bounced around from work to family and then, somehow, back to Christina. Blair asked about the mission foundation, and Dexter coughed out a plethora of information. Blair was impressed with the efforts he described, but beyond that, she was amazed at his level of involvement.

"How do you know so much about it?" she asked.

"Well, Christina keeps me posted," he revealed. "*And* I went with her to the children's hospital last month."

Blair leaned back in her chair and crossed her arms. "I see," she said with a slow grin.

"What?"

"Nothing."

"What do you see?"

"Nothing," she said again. "Just that you have the 4-1-1 on a matter that's important to you. And directly from the source. The very *attractive* source."

Heat flooded Dexter's face. In an attempt to camouflage it and gather his wits, he took a sip of his lemonade. "It *is* an important matter, and Christina *is* the source of my information."

"And...?" Blair prompted.

"You want to know if I find her attractive," he observed, and when she only smiled, he admitted, "Of course I do."

"You two are good friends, aren't you?" she acknowledged, backtracking to a tone without judgment.

"We have a lot in common," he said without elaborating.

Blair swallowed a bite of her sandwich, making the decision to drop the subject. Or so she intended. "You said you're eating out later; what do you have planned?"

"Going to Green Hollow later for dinner and a movie."

She raised an eyebrow. "By yourself?"

Dexter grinned. He might as well let the cat out of the bag. "I'm taking Christina," he revealed.

Blair chose not to give her big brother a hard time. She knew he'd had a tough time since Sarah had left. "Venturing into new territory?" she asked, "Or just going as friends?" Her tone was sincere, and it effectively coaxed a dose of honesty from Dexter.

"She's an amazing woman. I'm awfully fond of her. And I'm very happy to report that she's agreed to go on a date with me."

"That's wonderful, Dex."

He answered only with a smile. When they parted a few moments later, Blair elicited a promise from him to keep her posted. She longed for his happiness, and had a good feeling about Christina Sinclair. Blair would be rooting for Dexter and Christina.

~~~~~~~~~~

Dexter drove around the block twice before pulling into Christina's driveway, killing time so as not to be too early. Punctuality seemed like a big deal on this occasion. It was 5:30 on the nose when he rang her doorbell, a bouquet of fresh flowers in hand. He stood on the very porch where he and Christina had sat less than a week ago. He was clad in a polo shirt and jeans, having put a lot of thought into his choice of attire. He had told Christina that casual was fine so he hoped this would work okay with whatever she had on. Dexter heard footsteps approaching on the other side of the door and looked up just in time to see Christina open it wide. She greeted him with a radiant smile and a fragrant aura. She smelled fresh and citrusy, though not overpowering. She stood before him in a flowing summer dress. Her shoulders were bare and lovely, but she had a sweater draped over one arm.

Dexter presented the flowers, for which she gushed her gratitude. "Would you like to come in or are we ready to go?" she asked brightly.

"I'm ready if you are," he said.

"Let me just give these to Haley to put in a vase," Christina said, stepping away from the door only briefly. She was back in a matter of seconds and they were on their way.

Dexter open the vehicle door for her. As she got in, he said, "You look beautiful."

"Thank you," she replied, her cheeks warming.

With so many years since either of them had been on the dating scene, both Dexter and Christina were somewhat jittery. Fortunately, however, they had a foundation of friendship that eased the progression. Before he knew it, they were filling the SUV with chatter about family, Christina's meeting with the DOM, musical preferences, food choices, etc.

Dexter's heart skipped a beat when, at a point of animated conversation, Christina laid a warm hand on his forearm and threw her head back in laughter over something he'd said. The sound of her mirth and the warmth of her touch made Dexter feel alive in a way he hadn't realized was possible.

They made a restaurant choice and were seated promptly. Dexter loved that Christina had an adventurous palette, not shying away from the spicy appetizer he suggested. And Christina loved that Dexter was so easy-going about things. She wondered briefly if that would change after the novelty wore off, but with the advantage of a solid friendship, Christina believed that he was genuine and congenial as a rule. And he certainly smelled nice!

"I think I want bleu cheese crumbles on my steak," he said. "It's an add-on option."

"Wonder how it would be on the grilled chicken?" Christina asked.

"You can't go wrong with bleu cheese on grilled meat as far as I'm concerned.

"I'll try it then," she said decisively.

Dexter marveled at her willingness to try new things. Sarah would've not only turned her nose up at "moldy cheese," but also made him feel deviant and gross if he'd eaten it in front of her. This was such a refreshing change! He knew that it wasn't a good idea to compare Christina to Sarah, but to some extent, it couldn't be helped. One couldn't just ignore his point of reference. He was sure it was the same for Christina, and that thought made him wonder how he stacked up against Anthony. He quickly chased that thought away.

Their meal was delicious, but as with many new couples, they didn't eat quite as heartily as they might have otherwise. The timing didn't work out quite right for the movie they wanted to see. Instead the couple found themselves walking the square in the center of Green Hollow. It was well-lit, quaint and charming -- and filled with others who were strolling. Jazz music from a nearby cafe offered an ambience conducive to romance. One oblivious couple was swaying to the music near a beautiful fountain. Dexter and Christina strolled, hand in hand, around the square. They walked, and they talked. And then they sat on one of many benches, easy conversation flowing between them. It felt so good to be with someone in this way, to have Christina on his arm. It was such a natural fit when he took her hand that all their earlier apprehension had disappeared. For these few hours, Dexter forgot his worry over why his marriage had failed. He set aside thoughts about how he compared to Anthony Sinclair. He ceased to stress about whether he was moving things along at a pace that was acceptable for the widow that Christina was. Dexter was simply caught up in the pleasure of Christina's company.

Unbeknownst to him, Christina's enjoyment of the evening came only after a pep talk from her pastor's wife, Melissa. Christina's last-minute doubts had almost caused her to cancel their plans. Her ambivalence about embarking on a new level of involvement with Dexter was put to rest when Melissa assured her that it was not disrespectful to Anthony's memory or the love they shared if Christina found happiness with someone else. Haley said something similar, telling her mother, "Mom, we all know you'd be with Daddy if he was still here -- but he *isn't*." So with some coaxing from her friend and the blessing of her children, Christina set aside her concerns and allowed herself to enjoy the evening.

And it was a *splendid* evening -- filled with the familiarity of an old friendship, but topped with an icing of possibility and wonder. When Dexter arrived at Christina's home to drop her off, he was sad to see the evening at an end. His heart felt the disappointing void at the very thought. Still, the evening had to end in order for others to begin. Dexter walked Christina to the door, where she thanked him for such a nice time.

"It was my pleasure," he replied, adding, "Truly."

"Talk to you tomorrow?" she asked coyly.

"Of course," he said, his eyes crinkling with a smile. He gave her hand a squeeze and leaned in to kiss her cheek. He wanted very much to kiss her lips, but it felt right to wait. Christina didn't exhibit any outward signs of nervousness, but tilted her head slightly to offer her cheek, confirming that Dexter's decision was the right one. It had been a lot of years since either of them had been with anyone new in this capacity, and he knew slow was the way to go.

That didn't stop his mind from racing ahead though. Dexter had to work super hard to keep his thoughts reeled in. His mind wandered to possible conversations, future dates, bolder kisses. In the days that followed that first date, no topic arose without Dexter wondering what Christina's opinion would be. Every song that played made him wonder if she liked it. Everything he ate evoked a curiosity about her favorite foods. He couldn't even sit down to watch television without texting her to see if she had seen that particular program. He was hungry for everything there was to know about her. He simply could not get enough of Christina Sinclair.

Chapter Eight

The summer was magical, with all the sparkle and wonder that comes with falling in love. Dexter, who had once believed he would never again risk opening his heart, was falling in love with Christina. He worked alongside her as she tirelessly perpetuated their mission efforts. He marveled at her compassion and selflessness. He enjoyed getting to better know each of her children: Jordan and his wife, Brianna; Haley and her boyfriend, Jared; and Payton and his girlfriend, Lily.

Likewise, he incorporated Christina into *his* family activities, though in all honesty, he was still a little leery about having her around Spencer. Christina seemed skittish too, cautiously gravitating toward his sister, Blair, and Spencer's wife, Paula. She and Paula were already good friends, having been neighbors for years. Everyone, it seemed, was happy to witness Dexter and Christina as a couple.

With so much family involvement and so much time devoted to mission work, actual *dates* and alone time were rare occurrences. Dexter had made every effort to follow Christina's lead on how to progress with their relationship. He was getting antsy though, he had to admit. They were halfway through summer, and had become quite comfortable with hand-holding and occasional hugs -- but he had yet to kiss her properly! And he was longing to.

When Christina suggested a weekend journey to Green Hollow for a concert, Dexter was thrilled. "It may be late when we get back," she said.

"What? Do you turn into a pumpkin or something?" Dexter joked.

"No... well, at least I don't think so anyway. It's been awhile since I was out past eleven."

"Me too," he laughed, adding, "but I think we'll be fine."

"Yes," she agreed. "We might even indulge in some porch-sitting when we get back."

He caught her gaze and then remarked, "Everyone else might be asleep when we get back."

Christina blushed, agreeing, "They might be."

Nothing more was said about it, but nothing more had to be. Dexter's imagination ran wild with the prospect of claiming her lips with his. A kiss like he had in mind would cement their status as an official couple. He had to be careful not to get carried away. Christina had stolen his heart, and he was attracted to her in *every* way. But what they had was something special -- maybe even God-ordained. He wanted to treat their relationship, and indeed, Christina, with respect. His intentions were honorable -- though admittedly, it was a struggle to keep his thoughts pure.

By the night of the concert, Dexter was striving to even care about the music. Though the concert was exceptional -- a local symphony that played orchestral renditions of pop hits -- his attention was on Christina and the tasteful blue dress she had on. It was the color of sapphires and it did something spectacular for her eyes. She caught him staring on more than one occasion.

"What?!" she asked, laughing as a hint of color rose to her face.

He leaned in closer, nuzzling her ear briefly before kissing her cheek. He rested his forehead against her head, his mouth hovering near her ear, "You are absolutely stunning," he intimated. "I can't keep my eyes off you." Dexter didn't see the way her eyes closed in response, but he *felt* her melt a little and knew that he was affecting her like she was affecting him.

If there had been any doubt, it was removed a couple hours later when they were alone on her porch. "Do you want something to drink?" Christina asked. "Some lemonade?"

"And risk waking the family?" When she smiled, he found the courage to speak honestly. "You know I love your lemonade, but right now there's only one thing that sounds better. I want to kiss you, Christina. *Really* kiss you. And without an audience." He paused, watching his sincerity sink in as her smile faded from her eyes and morphed into something smoldering. "May I?"

Christina nodded wordlessly. Dexter closed the distance between them, his right hand going to the side of her neck with his thumb grazing her jawline. He took her mouth with his, and she submitted willingly. Her lips parted, permitting a tentative exploration. The fingers of his right hand were soon tangled in her hair and he realized he was using his left hand to pull her closer to him. Dexter was so hungry for her and the intimacy this brought that he practically had to *tear* himself away. He pulled back ever so slightly, releasing the unintentional pressure on the small of her back. He continued to explore her mouth delicately and Christina continued to allow it, even reciprocating.

After several blissful moments, and by unspoken mutual agreement, they pulled back from the kiss. Slow smiles spread across their faces. Words were not necessary to convey the sentiments that were exchanged between them as they stood there in the darkness, and for a long moment they remained silent. Dexter pulled

Christina into his arms. With her head resting on his chest, he willed the moment never to end. Dexter knew that he was hopelessly in love with her and realized that he never wanted to be without her. It was all he could do not to utter the words *I love you* as he bent to kiss the top of her head. Would it be too soon? Would it frighten her? Was she ready? Did she feel the same way? After their passions had taken the lead momentarily, would she mistake a proclamation of love as a ploy for greater carnal indulgence?

There were too many questions, too much at risk. And so, Dexter bit his tongue. When he trusted himself to speak, he said simply, "I could stay like this forever."

He felt her nod against him, concurring. "Let's sit," she said after a moment. They dropped gently onto the swing and when Dexter lifted his arm to envelop her once more, Christina leaned into him and laid her hand on his chest. They stayed that way for an hour or more, talking in hushed tones and relishing an intimacy almost as great as that of their earlier kiss. Both Dexter and Christina were loath to end the night, but the chill of the eventide and the fact that they had church the next morning necessitated it. They had taken to visiting one another's churches, unofficially taking turns. Having previously established the next day's attendance at Helping Hands, Christina tilted her face up to his and asked, "See you in the morning?"

"You bet."

"I had a great time tonight."

"I did too," he said, smiling. He lowered his head to kiss her. Ten minutes later, they were *still* parting. It was an hour before Dexter fell into his bed wearing a smile and already looking forward to morning.

~~~~~~~~~

Dexter met Christina at church. As seemed to be the norm, she took his breath away. Was there anything she owned that wasn't flattering? How was he supposed to keep his focus on the sermon? Dexter had always acknowledged that Christina Sinclair was an appealing woman. She wore an attractiveness that was accessorized by her kindness. That was very appealing. Lately, however, he was acknowledging a lot more. Dexter saw an outer beauty that had been softened but not diminished with age. He found her to be extremely desirable, not only physically, but also spiritually. Dexter was drawn to her like a magnet. He wanted more of her. He craved her opinion on every matter. He *desired* her company regardless of what he was doing.

He *had* to let her know how he felt. She needed to know that she had his heart. The thought that she might not feel the same way was unbearable, but he had to know. As scary as it was, he figured it was better to know before he fell any deeper. Feeling suddenly brave, and admittedly *un*focused on the sermon, he doodled on the edge of his sermon notes.

DB <3 CS

He showed it to her, holding his breath. She glanced up at him and smiled. Taking his pen, she wrote

CS <3 DB

Dexter released the breath he'd been holding. Relief flooded him, and his heart soared. He grinned at her, and took her hand in his. They had been reserved about public displays of affection, but he threw caution to the wind. At that moment, he wanted to announce to the world that he loved Christina Sinclair and that he was the most blessed man on earth because she loved him back! He didn't, of course, but it wouldn't have taken much prompting.

After that, Dexter and Christina did nothing to hide the fact that they were a couple. She had her family's blessing, and he had his. And more importantly, they both felt confident that they had God's blessing on their courtship. Before long, their declarations of love for one another, verbal and face to face -- or by text message or on the phone, flowed freely.

Their summer proceeded with much busy-ness related to the missionary work. Jared had pitched in just like Dexter did, impressing both Dexter and Christina. Jared never had to be asked to do anything. He was just automatically there alongside the Sinclairs. Dexter agreed with Christina's observation that he was a great addition to the team.

"And what about to the family?" Dexter asked.

"He fits in very well, don't you think?" Christina replied, turning to look up at him.

"I do," he said, smiling.

"What?"

"Nothing. I just think maybe he's around for the long haul."

"That's my impression, too," she agreed.

"How do you feel about that?"

Christina sighed, gathering her thoughts before answering. "You know, as soon as I realized I was pregnant with each of my children, I began to pray for them. I prayed for them to be healthy and happy, to grow up loving the Lord... and I prayed for the spouses God had chosen for them. I have a feeling Jared is the one I've been praying for all these years."

"That's incredible," Dexter muttered.

"What do you mean?"

The fact that Christina didn't even know she was incredible was endearing. "I think a lot of people pray for their children to be healthy and happy. But to think ahead to their future and to know God well enough to know He is already there with a plan for them... and to pray for their spouses before you could even picture them as adults...Christina, that's amazing!"

"I don't know about all that," Christina said, squirming under the praise. "I just did what seemed right."

"And that makes *you* amazing," he declared.

She shook her head. "You'd do the same thing."

"I'd like to think I would, but I don't know."

"Do you regret not having children?" she ventured.

"Not really," he answered honestly. "I used to wish things were different, but I think it worked out just like it was supposed to." How could he tell her that he'd realized God knew just what He was doing? Children would have suffered with his and Sarah's divorce. And Dexter felt certain that God was allowing the void to be filled by his involvement in the lives of Christina's children. He didn't know how to express everything that was going through his mind and decided that it was best to leave it at that for now.

Christina accepted it, not pressing for further explanation. She was quiet though. This made Dexter wonder what she was thinking. He could probably guess. They hadn't been in the habit of ignoring the elephant in the room, so he just put it out there. "I'm sure you wish Anthony could be here for all this."

She was quiet for a moment longer, but laid a reassuring hand on his knee. "I hate that he isn't here to witness the kids keep reaching milestones, but I know he's in a better place and... well, I think it's working out like it's supposed to."

Realizing that her words mirrored his own, Dexter felt a sense of... not exactly relief... but contentment. He was more sure than ever that God had a hand on their situation and that the Holy Spirit was bearing witness to God's plan. There was really no other way to explain the peace in their hearts and the congruency of their sentiments.

Dexter never would have been so bold as to believe God had taken Anthony so he could have Christina -- and certainly wouldn't have given voice to that thought. But it was obvious to him that God took loving care of each of them and had presented the opportunity for him and Christina to find love again -- with one another.

Christina's gentle voice brought him out of his reverie. "Are you okay, Dex?" She slipped her arm through his as they sat on the porch swing.

"I am," he answered with a smile. "I'm more than okay."

Christina answered only with a tender squeeze of his arm and the resting of her head on his shoulder.

"I love you, Christina."

"I love you too," she replied without lifting her head.

~~~~~~~~~~

Christina's suspicion proved to be accurate. Jared was a nearly constant presence all summer long, contributing to the mission work and winning the hearts of the entire Sinclair family. Haley juggled mission work, social life, and the lifeguard job she had resumed at the pool throughout the summer.

One Saturday afternoon in early August, Jared surprised Christina by showing up one Saturday when he knew Haley was working. He knocked on the door, just as a courtesy, as he simultaneously poked his head inside. "Anybody home?"

"Come on in," Christina answered. She came to a stop at the end of the hall, taking in the sight of her daughter's boyfriend. "Jared! Haley's at work."

"I know," he replied, looking oddly sheepish. "I actually came to see you."

"Oh?" Christina was confused, and her confusion was quickly followed with mild concern. "Is something wrong?"

"No," Jared said. He rubbed his hands anxiously on the front of his shorts, causing Christina to doubt his truthfulness. "I just wanted to talk to you."

"Okay, let's sit down," she said. "Can I get you something to drink?"

"Maybe in a minute." He sat down on the couch, and Christina took a seat across from him. She waited with a wordless smile. Jared grinned and then cleared his throat. "Christina," he began, "I know you haven't known me that long…" His gaze fell away from her and he studied his hands intently. "But you know that Haley and I met quite a while back."

"Yes…"

Jared met her gaze once more. "I love your daughter."

"I know you do. I can tell."

"I never want to be without her," he said. Christina offered a smile to encourage him to continue. "Haley is everything I've asked God for. She loves her family and God and *me*." He chuckled nervously, and then went on. "She is warm and compassionate and *virtuous*. Do you have any idea how rare that is on a college campus?"

"My Haley-bug is special," Christina agreed.

Jared nodded, tears suddenly glistening in his eyes. "I want to marry her." He hesitated, gauging her response. A smile was forming on her face. Encouraged, he went on. "May I have your blessing?"

"Oh, Jared! Honey, of course!" They rose and closed the distance between them, embracing.

"I'll take good care of her," he murmured over Christina's shoulder. "You don't have to worry about that."

"Of course," she replied, giving him a squeeze and then pulling back. "I don't doubt that."

"I have to say it. Your daughter is a gift from God, and I just want you to know that I'll treat her as such."

Christina chuckled. "You know a day will come when she may not seem like such a gift."

Jared grinned in response. "I know marriage isn't all roses and glitter," he said, "but I pray that I never lose sight of the fact that she is a gift in my life."

"Aw, Jared... You already have the secret to a successful marriage." When he tilted his head in question, Christina went on. "You cherish the love you've found and keep God in the center -- you two will be fine."

He nodded, smiling broadly.

"Do you have a ring already?" she asked.

"I do," he said, pulling a box from his pocket. He flipped it open and showed it to Christina.

"It's lovely!" she gasped, inspecting it closely. "Haley will love it." She handed the box back to him.

"I hope so." He stuffed the box back into his pocket. "You won't say anything, will you?"

Christina, of course, agreed not to say a word. Jared revealed plans to propose that night. Neither of them had any real doubts about what Haley's response would be. What an exciting time!

Chapter Nine

Haley returned to college in late August, as an engaged woman. Dexter found it heartwarming to witness the love and devotion between her and Jared. Jared had graduated from college in May. Haley lacked only one semester of coursework before finishing her degree with an internship that could be done locally (or anywhere, for that matter). It was looking like a small Christmas wedding.

Payton moved onto the campus of a community college in a neighboring town. He was home on the weekends to see Lily -- and *maybe* his mother. The Sinclair household was much calmer, however. Dexter found Christina to be much more relaxed and *available*. They spent evenings on the patio next to the firepit and enjoyed cooking together frequently. He and Christina had often remarked that cooking for one was one of the biggest adjustments to suddenly being on one's own. For this reason, they relished preparing and eating meals together.

On one particularly warm fall night, they grilled some pork chops and veggies and dined on the patio. Christina turned on the Bluetooth speaker. With no one else around, Dexter took Christina's hand and pulled her into a slow dance when the right song came on. They swayed back and forth in time with the music. It felt so right to have her in his arms. He kissed her tenderly as they continued to move to the rhythm. Again, Dexter felt that he could happily stay like this forever.

When a faster song came on, Christina pulled back and said, "I almost forgot to tell you -- I made your favorite dessert."

"*Dessert* is my favorite," he laughed.

"I think you like this particular one."

"Surprise me," he said.

"I'll be right back." As Christina went into the house, Dexter's phone buzzed with an incoming message. *Sarah?!*

Hey Dex

How long had it been since he'd heard a peep out of her?! He tried to recall. What could she possibly want? His curiosity was high, but he wasn't about to disrespect Christina by having a conversation with his ex-wife while they were together. Whatever it was could wait until later. He slipped his phone back into his pocket as Christina came back through the door.

She handed Dexter a plate. "Oh my goodness, is this what I think it is?"

"Only if you think it's peanut butter pie," she quipped.

"This was the first pie you ever shared with me. Remember that day?"

"Of course I do."

"I knew then that you'd be a catch!"

"Sooo... *that's* why you love me," she accused with an arched eyebrow and a twinkle in her eyes.

"Only one of *many* reasons," he said innocently, leaning in to kiss her.

"Mmm, you taste like peanut butter."

The message from Sarah was forgotten as his attention remained on Christina and her pie. Pie and lemonade, though exceptionally tasty, were trivial matters -- icing on the cake. But she *was* a real catch, and he intended to make sure she knew that, never doubted her worth. *...far more than rubies...* The verse from Proverbs

31 came from nowhere, dancing through his mind like they had danced on the patio. He made a mental note to read the entire passage later.

When they reluctantly parted later -- parting was getting harder and harder -- Dexter drove the short distance home with a song trying to crawl up into his memory. He turned the radio down in an effort to let it take root. But it was elusive. He pulled into his garage without having retrieved it. Once inside, Dexter changed clothes and settled onto his bed with his Bible and his phone. As he had resolved, he flipped the Bible open to Proverbs chapter 31. He read the entire passage, picturing Christina with every word.

10 [b]A wife of noble character who can find?
 She is worth far more than rubies.
11 Her husband has full confidence in her
 and lacks nothing of value.
12 She brings him good, not harm,
 all the days of her life.
13 She selects wool and flax
 and works with eager hands.
14 She is like the merchant ships,
 bringing her food from afar.
15 She gets up while it is still night;
 she provides food for her family
 and portions for her female servants.
16 She considers a field and buys it;
 out of her earnings she plants a vineyard.
17 She sets about her work vigorously;
 her arms are strong for her tasks.
18 She sees that her trading is profitable,
 and her lamp does not go out at night.

[19] In her hand she holds the distaff
   and grasps the spindle with her fingers.
[20] She opens her arms to the poor
   and extends her hands to the needy.
[21] When it snows, she has no fear for her household;
   for all of them are clothed in scarlet.
[22] She makes coverings for her bed;
   she is clothed in fine linen and purple.
[23] Her husband is respected at the city gate,
   where he takes his seat among the elders of the land.
[24] She makes linen garments and sells them,
   and supplies the merchants with sashes.
[25] She is clothed with strength and dignity;
   she can laugh at the days to come.
[26] She speaks with wisdom,
   and faithful instruction is on her tongue.
[27] She watches over the affairs of her household
   and does not eat the bread of idleness.
[28] Her children arise and call her blessed;
   her husband also, and he praises her:
[29] "Many women do noble things,
   but you surpass them all."
[30] Charm is deceptive, and beauty is fleeting;
   but a woman who fears the LORD is to be praised.
[31] Honor her for all that her hands have done,
   and let her works bring her praise at the city gate.

Dexter closed his Bible and then closed his eyes. Christina was a Proverbs 31 woman if he'd ever known one. It was then that the song he'd been chasing around his head finally allowed him to catch it. It was a hip-hoppy Christian song about the Proverbs 31 woman. He grabbed his phone to pull it up, but saw Sarah's message and realized he hadn't replied. Should he? Out of curiosity, more than anything else, he decided to tap out a message.

Hey. What's up?

It was only a moment before Sarah replied.

Not much. Just wanted to see how you are.

Dexter couldn't help it; she brought out something in him that wasn't very gracious.

Since when do you care how I'm doing?

He watched the screen as she read the message. There was no reply for a couple of minutes though. Finally…

Fair enough. I deserved that. I'm sorry about the way things went down with us.

What do you even say to that? *Oh, that's alright? No big deal?* Dexter pitched the phone on the bed and crossed his arms. He glanced down at his Bible, knowing that he should hear her out. In his spirit, he knew that. But in his flesh, he wanted to turn his back on her the way she had turned her back on him, on their marriage. If his life were a cartoon, he imagined the little angel and little devil would be sitting on opposite shoulders dueling it out. The internal conflict was significant.

He couldn't find it in himself to pretend that everything was okay and to keep the resentment completely out of the correspondence. Picking up the phone again, he tapped out **Why r u sorry now?**

Sarah's reply was swift and simple. **Distance = perspective**

Dexter didn't reply. Indeed, distance *does* bring perspective. He still wasn't sure he wanted to hear anything she had to say though. *God…* His heart cried out, though he had no idea what to ask. *Just keep Your hand on this situation. Help me not to say or do anything that would displease you.* Dexter felt a sense of calm settle over him, but no nudge to respond in a particular way. So he didn't reply.

He glanced again at his Bible, and was reminded once more of Proverbs 31 and the song it inspired. He followed through, this time, with pulling it up on his phone. He listened to it, to the lyrics. A catchy rap song that wasn't normally his favorite style of music, he remembered it from a youth leadership experience a few years back. He had emphasized how Christians are set apart (as a peculiar people -- where was that? 1 Peter?) and should hold high standards for their lifelong mate. The youth loved that genre of music. The song really drove his point home. Had there *ever* been anything Proverbs 31 about Sarah? Why hadn't he heeded his own advice?

Dexter mulled this over, feeling his failure all over again. Of course, Sarah had possessed potential to be a good wife, and *was* a good wife at one time. They had been happy for a while. He thought so anyway. Maybe he hadn't cultivated Sarah's potential. In truth, neither of them brought out the best in the other. And Dexter knew that he wasn't exactly spiritually mature when they first got together. Was he blinded by love? And then, on the heels of that thought, was the next one: *Am I blinded by love now? 'Cause Christina sure seems almost perfect...*

At the thought of her, Dexter reached for his phone. He tapped out a message much like the ones he sent most every night.

I <3 u, Christina. GN.

Her reply came quickly, bringing a smile to his face. I love you too. GN.

Christina's presence, her ready response, was such a comfort. Knowing that she was only a text message or a phone call away meant the world to Dexter. How had he managed without her in his life? And yet, this business with Sarah niggled the back of his mind. He wondered about her apparent change of heart and wrestled with what his response should be. Dexter sighed deeply and turned off the light. With his head on the pillow, he pictured himself packing up his divorce papers and cell phone messages. He visualized himself actually putting them into a box and placing it at Jesus' feet.

As sleep began to pull him under and the distinction between random thoughts and dreams became fuzzy, Dexter saw himself pulling the box away from Jesus's feet just before the Savior reached down to pick it up. Bible pages were blowing around in a sudden gust of wind, and somehow, Dexter knew that they were significant. Reaching up, he snatched a page from the air. *Proverbs 31.* Of course. Dexter clutched the box in one hand, the passage in the other. Suddenly, it seemed important to put the passage in the box. When he opened it to put in the Bible page, the divorce decree and phone with Sarah's messages lay there. As he watched, the ink faded from the papers and Sarah's message morphed into Christina's good night declaration of love. He placed Proverbs 31 in the box carefully. It was then that he noticed a tiny box in the corner of the larger box. Dexter pulled it out and opened it, revealing a beautiful but simple diamond ring. It wasn't Sarah's engagement ring. It was a ring he'd never seen before. Wondering at this, he placed it back in the box. As he was about to close the lid, he saw that the ink on the divorce decree had reformed. Only now, it was a marriage certificate. Dexter smiled to himself, and in the dream, felt the Savior's hand touch his shoulder as he closed the box. He looked up into Jesus' face and was met with a warm smile and a sense of peace. Dexter handed the box to Jesus, who took it with a nod and then turned to leave. Jesus turned back to wave. Dexter raised his hand to mirror the gesture. And then it was over.

Dexter would struggle for days to put together remembered bits and pieces of that dream, but with limited success. While the complete memory of the dream escaped him, the contentment that it yielded did not. He carried with him a bit of comfort, a peace about the dissolution of his first marriage and a hope for the future with Christina. He even thought he might be able to leave his relationship with Sarah in the past while listening to what she had to say. Maybe, he thought, it would even *help* them move forward.

Dexter decided not to initiate contact with Sarah, but if she contacted him again.... Well, he would listen.

Chapter Ten

It wasn't like the idea hadn't already started to form in his mind. In all honesty, Dexter had fallen head over heels in love with Christina and couldn't imagine a future without her in it. If the seed had been planted of love's own accord, then Jared and Haley's engagement provided a little shot of Miracle-Gro and a nice drink of water. Love was in the air, and Dexter wanted to claim Christina as his own.

But they had only officially been a couple for a few months. Would she think it too soon? This whole thing had started with him being careful not to scare her off by moving too quickly. He surely didn't want to ruin it now! So Dexter didn't rush. He sat back and gnawed on the idea, figuring it might be best to wait until Haley's wedding was behind them and...well...a little more time had passed. There was a ring in that dream though, and it *had* to mean something.

It was a few days before he heard from Sarah again. Dexter had almost put her back out of his mind. But there she was, with a text message saying that she really needed to talk to him.

What do you need? He tapped his reply out impatiently.

Her reply came a few moments later. **To talk. F2F.**

Face to face?! She wanted to get together?! What in the world could she possibly want?

IDK, he stalled.

Please, Dex. I need to explain some things.

His first thought was Christina. He knew that Christina had his heart and that he had no romantic interest in his ex, but he didn't know how she would perceive it. He tried to imagine how he would feel if the tables were turned. He didn't like the thought of her meeting up with some other guy with whom she had a history, but he'd feel a whole lot better about it if she were up front with him about it.

U should know that I'm seeing someone. I don't want to do anything to make her feel uncomfortable.

He watched for the indicator that the message was delivered and then read. He waited for Sarah's response, imagining her digesting this news. He wondered whether she had considered this as a possibility. It was five whole minutes before he could see that she was formulating a message. When it finally came, it was surprisingly simple and uncharacteristically considerate.

I understand. I won't jeopardize your relationship. You deserve happiness. She can come too, if necessary. Just lmk.

Um...okay. Dexter actually double-checked the contact information to make sure the messages were coming from Sarah's number. He scratched his head. I'll talk to her.

Thanks, Dex. Hope to hear from you soon.

Wow. What an interesting development! Dexter hadn't expected Sarah to be so understanding about the courtesy he felt compelled to give Christina. He would have done the same toward Sarah if the situation had been different. It was only right to keep everything on the table so there were no misunderstandings.

He was in no hurry to see Sarah, but was curious about what she might have to say. He would run it past Christina later that evening, he decided. And if she had any reservations about it at all, then there would be no meeting. Dexter wanted a future with Christina and knew that had to be built on a foundation of love and trust -- with plenty of Jesus right in the middle!

~~~~~~~~~~

Christina's expression was unreadable. "She said you could come along if that's how we wanted to handle it," Dexter offered, handing her the bowl of chili he'd just ladled out for her.

She took the bowl, perching on a stool at his kitchen island. "Wow." Again, he couldn't tell what that meant. He brought his bowl over to the island as well, and busied himself with shredded cheese and saltine crackers.

Christina took a tentative bite of chili. "Mmm, this is *really* good!"

Dexter regarded her, his own dinner momentarily on hold. He stood with his arms broadly supporting his weight, hands on the island countertop. "I don't have to do this," he said. "That chapter of my life is finished, and the door can stay closed."

Christina took a careful drink of her cola and then met his gaze. "You feel she's sincere though," she observed, "and must be curious about what she has to say."

"Curious, yes," he said, nodding. "I can't imagine what she could really have to say. And there *does* seem to be something… different."

Christina stirred her chili around in her bowl. Finally, she sighed and looked up at him again. "I think you should go."

"Are you sure? Do you want to go too?"

She shook her head. "No, this is between the two of you."

"There is no *two of us* now though," he declared. "The only *two of us* that I'm a part of is the one that includes you."

"I know that, Dex," Christina said kindly. "But I wasn't on that part of your journey with you. And just because I wasn't there doesn't mean we should pretend it didn't happen. It *did*. You were married. And your former spouse is still around; it's a little different from my situation. If you can get some *c & c*, I think you should."

"C and C?"

"Clarity and closure," she said with a grin.

Dexter chuckled. Some clarity and closure *would* be nice. "But you don't mind me talking with her alone? It seems a little… I don't know… inappropriate. I don't want to disrespect you."

Christina smiled across the island at him. "I know that about you. I know that you don't want to disrespect me, and I know that you'll always, *always* be found trying to do the right thing. In fact, I know that I have your heart, and don't worry about old feelings for Sarah being rekindled so much as I might be afraid that her contrition may rouse up a sense of duty to give it another try or something." She let her gaze fall away from his and laughed softly, somewhat nervously, as if she only just realized that threat as it came out of her mouth.

"Hey," Dexter began as he rounded the island and closed the distance between them. He lifted her chin gently and locked eyes with her. "I owe Sarah nothing. Believe me, the Lord and I have had a *lot* of conversations about this. I gave it my all while we were together, kept praying and kept trying even after she left, went to counseling, and everything. She may or may not be sorry, but that doesn't change the fact that this ship has sailed. I don't feel obligated to give her a chance at anything other than *maybe* explaining what was going on with her at the time."

Christina blinked back tears, nodding. "Okay," she said.

"But you *were* right about one thing," Dexter said. When she looked at him expectantly, he continued, "You *do* have my heart."

"And you have mine, Dex." She stretched up to kiss him by way of confirmation. He returned her gesture, ending the kiss with a warm embrace. Christina's observation that their chili was going to get cold broke the intensity of the moment. They resumed their meal, setting aside thoughts of Sarah and her request.

~~~~~~~~~~

A week or so went by with no word from Sarah. Dexter scrolled back through his messages to see how he had left things with her. He thought he had left the ball in her court, but realized that she was probably waiting to hear from him. It felt a little wrong to be initiating contact with another woman, but supposed it wasn't right to leave

Sarah hanging either. And he *did* have Christina's permission. So, he tapped out as benign a message as he could manage.

Hey, I talked to Christina. If you still want to talk, she doesn't have a prob with it. If not, it's all good.

He read back over it before he hit send. He felt good about giving her an out. Maybe the notion had passed. If it had, so be it. He sent the message and laid the phone aside while he shifted his attention to some chores he'd been neglecting around the house. When he picked it back up twenty minutes later, there was no reply. Dexter shrugged and thought *well, I've done my part.*

Blair showed up a little while later, much to Dexter's surprise.

"Little Sis!" he greeted her as she came through the door. She had knocked, but was already on her way in before he could react. He'd have it no other way, and often did the same thing at her house.

"Hey stranger!"

"You're a sight for sore eyes. Come on in!"

"I thought I'd come see you since you're obviously too busy courting to come see me," she teased.

"Aw, is someone feeling neglected?" he cooed.

"Blood is supposed to be thicker than water... that's all I'm saying."

Dexter chuckled. "Okay, okay -- I have been a little tied up, I guess," he conceded.

Blair plopped down onto the couch, and Dexter offered her a bottle of water. "That's about all I have," he said regretfully.

"What? No time to shop either?! Things are worse than I thought!"

He arched an eyebrow at her. "Do you want the water or not?"

"Nah, I'm good."

The pair of siblings caught up on this and that, with the conversation eventually coming around to his ex-wife. "I hear there's trouble in paradise," she said.

Dexter regarded her, striving to keep his expression blank. Given recent events, he was curious. Naturally. But he had never had much use for gossip. He remained neutral, neither encouraging Blair to go on nor forbidding her to. Of course, if he were completely honest, he knew his sister would divulge more if he didn't stop her. Still, Dexter only shrugged.

"Every marriage has its ups and downs," he stated blandly.

"Oh, come on! Don't you want to gloat a little?"

He looked at her. *Of course*, his flesh wanted to gloat a little...indulge in a little *serves her right.* But he knew better than to nurture that part of himself. Besides, if Sarah hadn't ended their marriage, he could have never found love with Christina. Maybe it worked out like it was supposed to. He *was* curious, however, as to whether there was a connection between this development (if it was even true) and Sarah's desire to meet up.

"How do you even know?" he challenged.

"Well," she said, folding her legs up in under her, as if settling in for a good story, "My friend, Jade...you remember her, don't you? She was at Beth's Bistro last week and overheard Sarah's friend...what's her name? Anyway, she was on the phone. Jade's almost positive she was talking to Sarah. She said...."

"Blair!"

She stopped, looking at him innocently. "What?"

"That's gossip."

Blair let out a breath of resignation. She pursed her lips and glared at Dexter. "Why do you always have to be such a goody-two-shoes?"

"Why do *you* always have to be such a gossip?"

"But Jade *heard* her *say*..."

Dexter held a hand up, effectively stopping her in her tracks. Normally, he would have been inclined to confide in his sister about Sarah contacting him. Not now though. It would only add fuel to a barely-contained fire.

"It doesn't matter," he said simply.

"But don't you...."

"Just let it go, sis."

Blair crossed her arms, making a show of pouting. "Okay," she said dramatically.

Dexter couldn't help but chuckle. "This side of you isn't very attractive," he observed lightly, at which point she hurled a throw pillow in his direction.

"*None* of your sides are very attractive," she declared, ducking as he tossed the pillow back toward her.

His sister was great -- always a good sport and could give as well as she could dish out... and could even be a good confidante when it mattered -- but she *was* prone to gossip. That was one of the biggest differences between the two of them. Dexter had always found gossip more than merely a little distasteful. Even when rumors were true, and were known to be fact, idle talk just kept things stirred up. His motto was that if it wasn't his story/secret to tell, he didn't like to tell it. Blair had no such motto, he mused.

It was after Blair left that Dexter thought to check his phone, finding the reply from Sarah.

I do still want to talk. When and where?

When and where, indeed. It was the *where* that bothered him. He wanted enough privacy to be able to talk, but didn't relish the idea of being completely alone with her. There was no need to provide such an opportunity for rumors. He thought for a minute. Surely there was a solution. Meanwhile, he tapped out a response.

When would you be available?

Her reply was immediate, indicating that she was available any afternoon that week. Dexter inquired as to her ideas about where to meet. Sarah texted back that she could come over or he could come by her place. Out of curiosity, Dexter asked Would your husband be okay with that?

She simply said We'll work it out.

I'll get back to you in just a little bit.

K.

An idea was forming in his mind. Dexter dialed Pastor James' number. When the man picked up, Dexter explained the situation and that, naturally, he had reservations. "I feel like I need to hear her out, for her sake *and* for mine. I don't want to invite gossip though, and don't feel like it would be a good idea to be completely alone….yet we need privacy to talk Do you suppose we could meet at your office?"

"Of course, I don't mind. Do you think Sarah will go for it? She hasn't graced our doors since before you two split up. This is bound to feel like *your* territory."

"I don't know. We'll see. Just wanted to run it by you first. She says she can meet most any afternoon. When would it be the least inconvenience for you?"

The pastor indicated that Wednesday and Thursday afternoons would allow for him to give up use of his office for an hour or two. Dexter thanked him and ended the call. After tapping "end," he tapped out the offer to Sarah. Much to his surprise, she agreed without hesitation. Within moments, it was all arranged. They would meet at the church building at 4:00 on Thursday. Now, there was nothing to do but wait...and pray that it would go well.

Chapter Eleven

"I just want you to know that I was in a very bad place when this all started," Sarah began.

"What do you mean?" Dexter asked, shifting in his chair.

"I felt like there was something wrong with me, and I didn't know how to talk to you about it."

"Go on."

Sarah took in a deep breath and released it. "I know you've figured out that I was involved with Mark before I actually left. I hope someday you can forgive me for that." She had been studying her fingers anxiously, but lifted her eyes then to meet his briefly. He didn't say anything. She went on. "I guess it all started years ago with Spencer."

At that, Dexter was out of his chair. "You had something going with my *brother*?" he demanded.

"No! Please, sit down and listen." He regarded her, considering. "Please."

He did not sit. Not yet. "What do you mean that it started with him then?"

"We both know your brother strays. That isn't news, Dex."

"Well, you know...none of us can figure out why. Right? I mean, he seems crazy about Paula, doesn't he?"

Dexter was nodding. His brother's behavior *was* puzzling. But... "Did he try something with you? Did..."

Sarah shrugged. "There were always innuendoes. I don't know if it would've gone further than that if I had let it or not."

Dexter stewed. His own brother! What kind of a guy doesn't have enough respect for his own flesh and blood not to consider his wife off limits?! "Why didn't you say anything?"

"He was bad about misconstruing things. And maybe I *did* get a little flirty a time or two. But he would have made it sound like it was all me. Either way, it would have just caused trouble in the family. So I just stayed away from him unless you or Paula was around."

"I can't believe him. I gave him more credit than that."

"He's your brother, Dex. Your very *flawed* brother," she said, chuckling dryly. "But he has a lot of good qualities, and I didn't tell you this to make you angry at him."

"Why *are* you telling me this?"

"It's just part of the background, I guess. I've thought so much about this, trying to piece it together myself. I know you deserve an explanation too, so I just want to share the factors that set the stage for what happened." She left that hanging in the air for a moment, waiting for eye contact or some indication that she should continue.

Finally, Dexter said, "Okay. I'm listening."

"Over the years, I wondered what made Spencer stray from Paula. You and I even talked about it once, remember? I remember thinking that something must just be missing for him, something that he couldn't find in his marriage. Not that Paula was lacking in any way... just that...I don't know. But those were the thoughts in the background. And then there was the baby issue." She stopped there, studying her hands again. Dexter didn't interrupt. He just waited. "I've never been a super-nurturing person," Sarah rejoined. "I wasn't one of those little girls who played with dolls and daydreamed about having babies one day."

"I didn't push," Dexter offered quietly, trying to put it all together.

"No, you were great," she acknowledged, "but I know you would have liked to have had children." She paused, locking eyes with him. "You would be a great dad." She sighed. "I'm sorry I deprived you of that."

"This is all water under the bridge, Sarah."

"But I kind of felt like something was wrong with me. You know? I mean, most women have some kind of instinct that kicks in and they want to procreate with the man they love."

"Did you even love me?" he asked before he could stop himself.

"I did. But maybe not like I should have... well, obviously." Dexter chuckled a little at that. She offered a weak smile. "What I mean is... I guess I had fallen *out* of love. I don't think that's uncommon in a marriage....falling in and out of love. It's what you do with it that matters. I know that I didn't take care of our love, our marriage. Then when Mark came along and started paying so much attention to me, I couldn't see anything but your flaws, the flaws in our marriage. And I got to thinking that maybe the maternal instinct hadn't kicked in because I wasn't with the right person. Spencer has been cheating for years, and I thought that maybe monogamy was just idealistic. Maybe everyone cheated, but most are more discreet. My thinking got so screwed up. Before I knew what was what, I was pinning my hopes on Mark. The more I fell for him, the less satisfied I was with us." She waved a finger between the two of them and let out a defeated breath. "I realize now that I wasn't putting anything into our marriage and couldn't have expected to get anything out of it."

"Wow," Dexter offered with no clue what to add to it. He had so many thoughts, but had no idea how to articulate them. It probably wasn't a good idea to try anyway.

Sarah gave him a moment to digest what she had told him, but could stand it no longer. "Well?" she prompted.

He looked at her, this woman he had vowed to love and honor until death parted them. This woman who, by her own admission, had been unfaithful and *then* decided to leave him. He recalled the confusion he felt at their constant arguments. He remembered wondering where he had gone wrong, what had brought about the change in her attitude. He grieved at the ending of their marriage, but more than that, he had struggled with so much guilt. Unnecessary guilt. And now that she was finally willing to talk with him, it didn't make much more sense than it had then.

"You were so bitter," he finally ventured. "I couldn't get through all the hostility to find you and figure out how to fix things."

"I'm sorry, Dex. Honestly, I knew that if I let you in enough to talk about things, even if I opened up about where things were heading with Mark, you would have been bent on trying to work it all out. You would have tried to stop me from leaving. You would have preached to me about marriage being for life. I didn't want to stay, and I couldn't let you try to make me."

He stared at her in disbelief. "*You* made up *your* mind about *our* marriage, *our* future. And you couldn't risk me pointing out that we took vows before God? You shut me out to try and avoid a guilt trip?!" His voice was only slightly elevated. He thought he'd done a remarkable job at keeping his cool. "How had that worked out for you, Sarah?" he spat.

"I know I was in the wrong," Sarah admitted. "I was wrong in my thinking, in my actions, for getting involved with Mark, for shutting you out, for breaking my vows...I was wrong!" Hot tears streamed down her cheeks.

Dexter's anger slipped a little. He never could stand to see a woman cry. There's nothing in the world that could undo what had been done. Though her logic was faulty and her actions wrong, he knew that there was nothing she could do or say to take it back. All either of them could do was move forward from where they were now. And it would accomplish nothing to make her feel worse when she was attempting to make amends. He heaved in a long breath and let it out. "Was it worth it?" he asked softly. "Are you happy?"

Sarah sniffled and choked out something between a sob and a humorless laugh. "Well, one would hope so after all that I've put us through." Dexter offered a sad smile, but said nothing. She chewed the inside of her jaw pensively. "Mark's a pretty good guy, but I can never forget the circumstances we fell in love under and I wonder if we'll ever fully trust each other."

Dexter nodded sympathetically. "I've learned a few things along the way though," she went one.

"Oh yeah? What's that?"

"When the grass seems greener on the other side of the fence, it's time to start tending to the grass on your own side. Every relationship comes with its own set of problems. I can't change the way yours and mine turned out, but I'll be found trying my best with Mark. It's all I know to do."

He nodded. "I guess you're right."

"I truly am sorry for the pain I put you through. If it's any consolation, I will pay for it every day the rest of my life. You have no idea what it's like to wake up every morning and know that I was *that* woman, that I'm the one who cheated. Do you think you'll ever forgive me?"

"I don't hold it against you, Sarah. I wish you happiness."

"What about you? Christina Sinclair, huh?" she asked with a smile. "Are you finding happiness?"

"I am," he said simply, holding back the part about how the happiness he'd found with Christina made all the heartbreak worth it and the forgiveness a little easier.

"I'm glad, Dexter. Really, I am."

With that, there didn't seem to be anything else to say. Dexter felt he had made the right decision by coming here. It really did feel good to have closure. He gave Sarah a light hug before she left and bid her farewell, effectively closing out that chapter of his life.

Pastor James caught him before he left, and Dexter lingered back to speak with the older man. "How did it go?" he asked Dexter.

"You know, it went well."

"Good, good. Did you gain any insights?"

"Yeah, I suppose I did. She owned up to some things and explained her frame of mind that led to some wrong decisions."

Pastor James nodded thoughtfully. "You know, the good Lord saw fit to allow us free will. I believe that His hand of grace is all in the world that keeps us from making a royal mess of our lives every day. Every now and then, I think He lifts His hand of grace off us and just lets the free will thing play out. But He never leaves. He's always there. And He will always work it out for us when we keep loving Him."

"That's a great way to put it, Pastor. I know forgiveness is the way to go anyway, but it's hard to hold a grudge against her when I'd have never known the love I've found with Christina if Sarah had behaved."

"Beauty for ashes, son," Pastor James said, clapping Dexter's shoulder with a smile. "Beauty for ashes."

Chapter Twelve

Well, that was true, he supposed. Dexter replayed Pastor James' words as he drove home. He knew the passage to which he had alluded, and vowed to let that be his evening reading later. Meanwhile, he wanted to touch base with Christina. Dexter tried to imagine being in her shoes, waiting to hear how a conversation with a very real, very present, very *alive* ex had gone. It must be so very different. Dexter wondered sometimes how he measured up against Anthony's memory. Christina never openly compared the two of them -- she was too classy for that -- but their previous marriages couldn't help but provide a point of reference for each of them. He didn't intentionally compare Christina to Sarah, but was helpless not to acknowledge ways in which they were similar (few) and ways in which they were different.

The biggest difference Dexter had found with Christina was that she seemed to bring out the best in him. She was so easy-going and slow to anger. Being with her was easy. Dexter was not on the defensive like he constantly was with Sarah. And she was so well-grounded in God's word that it made it easy to be a better man, to do the right thing, to keep his priorities straight.

Dexter was certain that Anthony Sinclair had his faults. He was human, after all. But as far as he knew, Anthony was a terrific man. He had certainly been a terrific friend. And of course, Christina nor any of the children never spoke ill of him. Dexter worried that he paled in comparison. He could get bogged down in that if he wasn't careful. If Christina had any of the same insecurities in regard to Sarah, she didn't let on. But wouldn't they be even harder to shake with Sarah still being *around*. As great as Anthony was, he was gone, never to return.

These musings kept Dexter's mind occupied on the way to Christina's house. As he pulled into her driveway, he noticed several large potted mums lining the porch steps. Burgundy, yellow, rusty orange, and white -- so beautiful. These were new. As he lingered to admire them, Christina stepped through the door and onto the porch with a smile and two glasses of lemonade. Seeing him looking at the new flowers, she asked, "Do you like them?"

"They're gorgeous! You've been busy."

She handed him a glass. "Brianna and I bought those. I think every year that I'll set them out so I won't have to buy any the next year, but I never do. I never can decide where to put them, and somehow, planting flowers seems like a spring thing to do. Anyway, I've got some more for a fall display. You can help if you want or I can draft the guys if that's not your thing."

She was nervous, he thought. It wasn't like her to chatter on like this. He chuckled good-naturedly. "I'd be happy to help. It's sure looking nice so far," he said. He tilted his head toward the porch, inviting her to sit. As they settled onto the swing, he asked what sort of display she had in mind.

"Well, I have this big scarecrow, and I bought some pumpkins and Indian corn."

"We should get some hay bales," he offered.

"Yes!" Christina smiled, grateful that he was on board with helping decorate. She took a sip of her lemonade and leaned back. When Dexter followed suit, she asked how his conversation with Sarah went.

"It was interesting," he answered, not sure where to start. "It went okay."

"Did she provide any insight into what all has happened?"

"Some," he said. "I still don't really understand, but it seems like her thinking was just all goofed up. She said that she had started to think something was wrong with her because she didn't want children. And then when the guy she married started paying attention to her, she got to thinking that maybe the thing that was wrong was that she was with the wrong person."

"What?!" Christina exclaimed softly.

"I know. Even Sarah knows now that it didn't make much sense."

"Goodness."

"Oh, and she brought up my brother."

"No! They didn't..."

"I don't think so, though she said that he had tried to flirt with her some. She was saying that Spencer had been unfaithful so often that she got to thinking that maybe everybody was and that some just hid it better than others."

`Christina raised her eyebrows. "Sounds like she was looking for an excuse to misbehave, if you ask me!"

Both of them laughed lightly. "It does. And I think she recognizes it for what it is now."

"Hmm," Christina muttered thoughtfully.

"She asked me to forgive her. Said she hoped I had found happiness with you."

"And what did *you* say?"

"I told her that I wasn't holding any grudges and that I wished her happiness. I mean, how can I hold it against her when I've found something so much better with you. I'd never wish a divorce -- especially involving infidelity -- on anyone, but if it hadn't worked out that way, I might have gone a lifetime without knowing a love like ours." Dexter took Christina's hand and gave it a squeeze.

"Aw, Dex,"Christina replied with tears springing into her eyes, "Thank you for saying that; it means so much. And you know, I would have never chosen to be a widow. It's horrible to suddenly be without the person you've built a life with. I don't even know how to describe how adrift you feel, the loneliness and disillusionment. I wondered if I'd ever feel *whole* again. I was blessed to have the love of a good man for all those years, and I didn't dare to hope to have the love of another. But our God is a mighty and gracious one, and He sent you to me just when I needed you -- first as a friend -- no, first as a plumber..." Christina laughed through her tears, and Dexter chuckled as well, but waited for her to go on. "Seriously, you have been precisely what I needed every step of the way. When I needed help around the house, you were there. When I needed a friend, you were there. When I felt capable of opening my heart, you were there. I want you to know that I love you, Dexter Billings, and I thank God for you every single day."

Dexter folded her into his arms, overcome with emotion and relief. The words she had said were the perfect balm for a heart made fragile by an overactive mind. "I love you too, Christina, so much. And I'm so thankful for you, thankful that God brought us together." He hugged her tight, reluctant to let go, and there they stayed as night fell around them.

~~~~~~~~~

After a quick shower, Dexter settled onto his bed with his phone and his Bible, as was his habit. He liked to begin and end his day with the Lord and Christina. He used his phone to look up the passage he sought, but he opened his actual Bible to read the verses. He could study better that way. He turned the worn book to Isaiah, the 61st chapter.

"To console those who mourn in Zion,
To give them beauty for ashes,
The oil of joy for mourning,
The garment of praise for the spirit of heaviness;
That they may be called trees of righteousness,
The planting of the Lord, that He may be glorified."

He read and then re-read, digesting the words, promises that God would more than make up for the sorrows and hardships we suffer. He certainly had made good on this promise for Dexter. He picked up his phone and texted a simple **Isaiah 61:3** to Christina, then turned his attention back to his Bible. He made some notes and looked up some cross-referenced verses. Soon, his phone lit up with Christina's reply.

Oh my goodness. You won't believe it! I've had that passage on my heart so strong the past few days.

Dexter smiled at the way the Lord worked.

Doesn't surprise me a bit! GN. Love u.

Her reply, bidding him a good night and sweet dreams, returning his sentiments, came quickly and brought a contentment that was conducive to sleep.

When the weekend came, Dexter joined Christina to complete her fall decorations. Once he got into it, he totally went above and beyond what Christina had initially envisioned. He landed six bales of hay and a huge cluster of dried corn stalks. He and Christina bought more pumpkins and some Indian corn. Together they assembled a magnificent display of autumn splendor.

Sunset brought a chill that drove them indoors. Tired and hungry after working all afternoon, they opted for an easy, but satisfying meal of tomato soup and grilled cheese sandwiches. Effortless conversation flowed between the two of them, spanning Haley's wedding plans, the latest mission efforts, whether or not they should whip up a cobbler for dessert, and everything in between.

"Who will give her away?" Dexter asked regarding the upcoming wedding.

"I'm not sure," Christina answered. "We've talked about it, but haven't really decided. It's up to Haley, of course, but I thought Jordan might walk her down the aisle. When the question is posed, he could just indicate that her family gives her to be married."

"You could just leave that part out altogether," he offered.

"We could," Christina agreed.

"It will be a bittersweet day without her daddy, no matter what."

Christina sighed. "Yes, it will. But life has to go on, right?"

Dexter answered with only a sad smile before his phone buzzed. A text message from Blair invited them out to Sally's for pie.

"Well, that would solve our cobbler dilemma," Christina remarked.

"Do you feel like going?" When she answered in the affirmative, he added, "Even if Spencer and Paula are there? Whoever initiates a pie excursion usually invites everyone."

Christina laughed lightly. "As long as you and Paula are there."

"Sadly, I don't think I could ever intentionally leave you alone with my brother."

She planted a kiss on his cheek and said, "I'm glad you're nothing like him."

"And I'm glad you recognized that!"

"Let's go eat some pie!" Christina said, grabbing her jacket from the hook in the foyer. With that, they headed out the door.

~~~~~~~~~~

Blueberry pie, apple pie, and cherry pie were the flavors of the day. How American could this place get?! Every variety was represented around the table, and before it was over with, pretty much everyone had sampled each kind. "Well, I ordered cherry," Christina told Dexter, "but I think apple was my favorite."

"Apple's good," he agreed, "especially with ice cream."

Spencer leaned back in his chair, rubbing his stomach. "They're *all* good," he said. There was a murmur of agreement around the table. Sally's was a

Billings family favorite, and her amazing pies contributed mightily to that status.

The group was down to crumbs, refills on their coffee, and good-natured chit chat when Christina's phone buzzed. Glancing at the screen, she offered a general apology to the table and shared with Dexter that it was Haley. "Probably a wedding detail... you always *think* you can keep it simple." He chuckled his understanding and Christina stepped outside to take the call from her daughter.

When she was gone more than a couple of minutes, Dexter took Christina's jacket to her and mouthed to her an indication that he was going to pay the bill and would be back. As she ended the call in unison with the door opening a second time, Christina fully expected to see Dexter when she turned around. Instead, much to her dismay, she locked eyes with Spencer.

"Spencer..."

He smirked a little, noticing her discomfort. "I just came on out for a breath of fresh air," he offered in answer to the question she didn't ask.

"I was just heading back in," she said, moving to step around him toward the door. He shifted quickly though, blocking her way. She looked up at him, locking eyes again. "What are you doing, Spencer?" she bit out.

Mild amusement danced in his eyes briefly before it was placed with apparent sincerity. "We got off to a bad start..." he began. Christina crossed her arms defiantly. If he thought it was that simple, he was wrong. "I just wanted you to know that I'm happy for you and my baby brother."

Christina arched an eyebrow, saying nothing.

"Really, I am."

"That probably means a lot to Dexter." She watched as the unspoken suggestion that it meant nothing to her registered in his expression. Almost immediately, his expression became unreadable.

"I'm just curious though…" he said, taking a step forward. He was much closer than Christina would prefer -- and where was Dexter?! She looked around nervously, silently praying that Dexter or *any* member of the Billings family would come out that door. But no one did, and Spencer seemed to enjoy watching her squirm. He went on, "I just wondered why you're buying what he's selling -- I mean, I *was* there first." Spencer reached out to touch her face, running the back of a finger down her cheek. "You know I have a lot to offer."

Christina took a step back, outraged. She regarded him in cold disbelief. "Are you that stupid?"

Spencer clucked his tongue and donned a wounded expression. "There's no need for name-calling."

"First of all, Dexter's twice the man you'll ever be," she spat. "And second if you don't know that the fact you have a wife means that you have nothing to *sell* that I have any interest in *buying*, then yes -- stupidity is the only word for it."

The door opened behind him, and the remainder of the family began filing out. Dexter was at the front of the line, wearing a look of concern on his face. Spencer's voice took on a considerably lighter tone. "Like I was saying, I'm happy for you guys." And then with his eyes never leaving Christina's. "You two are *perfect* for each other."

Chapter Thirteen

Dexter walked briskly to Christina's side, offering a tight smile as he slipped a protective arm around her. How had Spencer managed to catch her alone? *Years of sneaky behavior maybe?* He called a "good night" over his shoulder to his family and with a firm hand on the small of her back, ushered Christina toward the vehicle.

"Is everything okay?" he questioned urgently as soon as they were seated and the doors were closed.

Christina wrestled with how much to reveal. She had held her own, she thought, and really didn't want to stir up trouble between Dexter and his brother. But she loved Dexter and didn't want to be dishonest with him. She stalled by answering in the affirmative, not supplying any specific information that hadn't yet been requested.

"Are you sure?" Dexter urged, his relief palpable when she smiled and confirmed her previous assertion. Only then did he start the ignition. Before shifting out of park, however, he said, "He's a sneaky one. I can't believe he ended up out there without me realizing it."

Christina chuckled uneasily. "It's no big deal."

"What was he doing out there anyway? Did he say?"

"Just that he needed a breath of fresh air."

Dexter harrumphed mildly as he pulled out of the parking lot. For a moment, he was lost in his own thoughts. Then he realized that Christina was uncharacteristically quiet. He glanced over in her direction. She was looking out the window. Dexter reached for her hand, which she gave willingly along with a weak smile. "Did he say anything out of line, Christina?"

She watched as his jaw tensed in the seconds before she answered. "Well, you know your brother can be a little rude. But he said he's happy for us."

Dexter wished it were daylight and that they were having this conversation face to face. Christina's answers seemed guarded, and his gut feeling told him there was more to it than what she was revealing. "What do you mean? What did he say that was rude?"

"Let's not spoil a good evening with all this talk about your brother, hmm?"

He took a couple of breaths. It was difficult to let it go without knowing exactly what Spencer had said. "I just need to know that...that you'd tell me if there's something I need to know."

Christina gave his hand a squeeze. "Of course," she said, flashing a quick smile.

"I love you," Dexter said quietly.

"I love you too," she replied. But then she turned back to face the window, staring out at the passing scenery without truly seeing it.

When they pulled into Christina's driveway, she didn't mention Dexter coming in. And it *was* getting late, he supposed. She stayed put until he walked around to open her door for her. He walked her to the door.

"Whew, that pie's about to put me in a coma," she commented as they neared the door.

"You should've ordered real coffee instead of decaf," Dexter teased.

"Remind me next time," she said, laughing lightly.

Dexter sought her gaze with his, lifting her chin gently with his hand. "Are you positive everything is okay?"

"Yes, of course." She tiptoed to plant a warm, reassuring kiss on his lips. She allowed the kiss to deepen somewhat in hopes of sidetracking him from the inquisition, but pulled back before they got carried away enough to suggest he come in for a make-out session. She needed to be alone with her thoughts. She needed to process and pray about this situation that had left her far more shaken than she was letting on. "Your kisses are one of my favorite things in life," she said sweetly. "They're the stuff sweet dreams are made of."

"So are yours, darlin'," he said, planting another one on her lips and murmuring *good night* against them.

"Good night, Dex," Christina said as he pulled back. "I'll see you at church."

"You bet."

~~~~~~~~~~

Dexter couldn't shake the uneasy feeling that had descended on him the moment he saw Spencer outside with Christina. It was a cloak of apprehension that weighed on him as he drove home, lingering as he showered and got ready for bed. What an appalling dilemma! He loved his brother, but hated his actions. Spencer truly had some wonderful qualities, but the fact of the matter was that Dexter didn't trust him alone with the love of his life. That thought saddened him deeply.

Maybe nothing had happened. Maybe Christina was only shaken because of being alone with him and worrying that something *would* happen. That, in itself, was sad. Many of Dexter's recent thoughts had revolved around the possibility of building a future with Christina. How could he convince her to share his life when that also meant sharing his family and being around Spencer, who obviously made her uncomfortable?

Dexter opened his Bible, but couldn't focus on the words of any particular passage. Finally, he gave up and closed the worn book. He sent a goodnight text message to Christina and closed his eyes, closed out the world as he approached his Father in prayer.

God, keep Your hand on this situation please. Don't let Spencer scare her off. Lord, I pray that You'll convict his heart and bring him into Your will. Thank You, Father, for Your blessings on Christina and me. I invite You into our relationship and pray that You'll help us not to do anything contrary to Your will.

His phone buzzed with Christina's reply, which he read with a smile. He turned off the light and pulled the bed covers up around him. Sleepily, he turned his attention back to the conversation with God.

Thank You for Christina. Thank You for bringing.... He was drifting off.

Dexter's last drowsy thought was a plea.

Don't let him run her off.

Across town, Christina was having her own conversation with the Lord… or at least *trying* to. She realized that she was having a hard time getting her heart in the right place to truly lift Spencer and Paula up in prayer like she needed to. Well, it wasn't so difficult with Paula. She prayed for Paula daily. With Spencer, however, it took a bit more effort...especially tonight. Christina knew that God's will was for her to turn the other cheek and to pray for her enemies. To say that was difficult to do was like saying there was a *little* water running over Niagara Falls. It was such an understatement that it was almost comical. What she wanted more than anything was for Spencer not to be an enemy. His behavior was so puzzling. Why couldn't he just be more like Dexter?

But he wasn't. As wonderful as Dexter was, he came with a family and that included Spencer. She was going to have to figure out how to deal with him and not live in fear of being caught alone with him. Either that or stop being around Dexter.

That thought brought an icy weight to her heart. Dexter's friendship had been a life preserver to which she had clung while adrift in a sea of grief. Christina truly felt like she would have drowned in her sorrow if he hadn't been there. Together, they coaxed one another along as they recovered from the blows they'd been dealt. And now….now, she had fallen in love with him. And not just a little bit. She was head over heals for the guy… something she never thought would happen.

The thought of not embracing that love felt like saying "no thank you" when God Himself was handing her a gift. No, she knew what a blessing Dexter was in her life. She would just have to learn how to handle his brother. But *how*?

God, I pray for Your blessing on Dexter and everyone in his life… including his brother. I pray that You'll equip me with enough courage and understanding to handle the vexation that surrounds this situation in a way that pleases You. Help me as I struggle to see Spencer as You see him, as Your child, as someone who is as deserving of Your love and compassion as I am, as a flawed individual in need of mercy.

When Christina began praying, it was out of frustration and a sense of duty. She didn't know what else to do, and she knew she was supposed to pray for her enemies. She was going through the motions. But as the words flowed out of her, she recognized the truth in them... Spencer *is* God's child. He *is* flawed and in need of mercy -- just like everyone else. She recalled a message she had heard at a youth rally one time. The leader began with making John 3:16 personal, having everyone to say it with their own names in place of "the world." Then he took it a step further and spoke of how Christians are called to love and pray for their enemies, instructing everyone to think of someone that could be considered an enemy and place *that* name in the verse.

For God so loved Spencer Billings *that He gave His only begotten son...*

That thought was sobering, and as she continued to pray, Christina began to *mean* it. She began to feel a peace in her heart that replaced the turmoil that previously resided there. As sleep began to pull her under, she relaxed in the assurance that this situation with Spencer was nothing God couldn't handle.

~~~~~~~~~~

There was no doubt God was on the case, nor that He could handle the situation. And though they didn't talk about it much, both Dexter and Christina could *feel* God working in their hearts individually as they strove to not let it interfere with their relationship. However, as often happens, things tend to get worse before they get better.

The weeks that followed were relatively uneventful, leading them right into the holiday season. As their families grew closer, and with wedding preparations in full swing, it was decided that their Thanksgiving meals would be combined. Dexter's family normally convened at Paula's while Christina's family joined her at home for the traditional feast. Christina still planned to contribute mightily to the cooking, but the Sinclairs would join up with the Billings family next door this year. Paula insisted on hosting in order to alleviate the stress of getting the house ready while cooking *and* tending to wedding details. She was so thoughtful that way, Christina thought. *Dear, sweet Paula.*

Dexter was all for it. He loved the notion of combining their family events. With one blaring exception, their families were a natural fit. Christina and Paula were dear friends, and Blair got along well with everyone. And Dexter was growing fonder of Christina's children all the time. Plus, it allowed him a glimpse of what it would be like if their families truly *were* combined.

He couldn't seem to get that thought off his mind. After achieving some closure with Sarah and having that visionary dream, Dexter had prayed and prayed about pursuing a life with Christina. He kept trying to bide his time until Haley's wedding was behind them; he truly didn't want to steal her thunder! But there was an idea brewing that he hoped to find time to speak with Haley about…

First things first though. Blair was contributing a couple of desserts and a casserole of some sort to the Thanksgiving meal. He told Paula that he'd bring drinks, but past experience had demonstrated the need for appetizers or something to munch on while the bird was cooking. He nearly starved to death waiting for it all to be done! So he was thinking of making some salsa and dip to bring, along with some chips and the drinks.

The list of dishes Christina planned to contribute was staggering, and she was so on top of it all that Dexter doubted she needed anything. Still, he shot her a text message before heading to the grocery store. When he got there, he found a reply indicating that she needed eggs and pecans. *Eggs and pecans*. He could do that.

When he stopped by to drop off the requested items, Christina was busy but not harried. Music played through a bluetooth speaker on the countertop and this woman that he loved was totally in her element. No less than four baking dishes could be seen through the oven door. Three of the four burners on the stove held pots that exuded enthusiastic steam. He looked around the kitchen in awe. The cutting board, currently in use, resided near the stove. Other counter space was occupied with pies and casserole dishes.

Christina paused long enough to receive a kiss on the cheek, taking the pecans from Dexter and instructing him to put the eggs in the refrigerator. When he opened the refrigerator door, he was stunned at the volume of food he found there -- deviled eggs, cranberry salad, some kind of dessert that involved whipped topping, something that looked like a salad or slaw. He turned around to Christina, who was already busily back to chopping onions.

"Is all this food for dinner at Paula's?" he asked incredulously.

"Only about half of it," she said. In the brief pause before she explained, Dexter was a little hurt at the thought that she might be planning a separate feast with only her own family. That thought barely registered before Christina cleared it up though. "The holiday committee from the foundation is organizing a Thanksgiving dinner for the families at the hospital. Normally the work would be more evenly distributed, but Sheila has flu running through her family and so many people are out of town. It was kind of a last-minute thing. They're coming by to pick up whatever I can contribute in a little while."

"Wow," he said. The mission foundation that Christina's family had established in memory of her late mission-minded husband was near and dear to all their hearts. It centered around a nearby children's hospital and the needs of its patients and their families. "I'd have helped more if I had realized all this was going on." Dexter had donated a half dozen cans of cranberry sauce and as many boxes of stuffing mix. His efforts seemed like nothing in light of the work Christina was doing here.

"I think it's all under control," she said. "It's going to be nice for the families to sit down together and have some sense of normalcy. They're going to decorate a room -- tablecloths, candles, the whole nine yards -- and serve up a respite from the world of sickness and worry. I kinda wish I could be there."

"Maybe at Christmas," he offered. "We're still considering that right? After the wedding?"

"Yes, definitely." Christina smiled at the memory of last year's first mission effort as a family -- reading stories to little ones, rocking babies while their parents got some rest, handing out gifts. It had been the perfect alternative to a traditional celebration without Anthony. Her heart and her family had come a long way since then. And so had the Anthony Sinclair Memorial Mission Foundation. Dexter had jumped right in and helped with their efforts, and had been touched by the children. She could hardly wait for him to experience Christmas with those little ones!

A knock at the door interrupted their conversation. "That'll be Alice here for the food."

"I'll let her in," Dexter said as he headed for the door.

They formed an assembly line with Christina retrieving the dishes she meant to send, handing them to Dexter, who carried them to the door and handed them off to the thin, pleasant woman. Alice placed them in her van. In the end, her van was laden with a large pan of dressing, two pumpkin pies, a chocolate cake, a tray of deviled eggs, a cranberry salad, a broccoli casserole, and two dishes of marshmallow-topped yams. All this was in addition to the three large pans of turkey, four pies, and assortment of vegetable and casseroles that were already in there. Alice and others had contributed generously. "Next stop, next door!" she said brightly as she got into her vehicle.

"Paula's contributing too?" Christina asked.

"She sure is!" Alice replied. "Two crock pots full of mashed potatoes, from what I understand. And a red velvet cake!"

"God bless that woman," Christina said, adding, "God bless all of you!! Happy Thanksgiving, Alice!"

"Happy Thanksgiving!" Alice called from her van.

Dexter put an arm around Christina's shoulder as they watched Alice pull out of her driveway and into Paula's. "I'm glad I got to witness that," he said.

Christina looked up into his face with a quizzical smile. "It does a heart good, doesn't it?"

"It sure does," he agreed. "Do you need me to do anything?"

"No, I think I'm on track. Thanks for the eggs and pecans."

"I'm going to run some things up to Spencer's and get the drinks iced down. I'll come back over in a bit. If you need me before you see me, just text."

Christina returned to the kitchen and Dexter headed next door. As she resumed the cooking, Dexter caught Alice in time to place a $100 bill in her hand. "For the last minute needs," he explained. Spencer, who was helping load crock pots, followed suit. With two hundred unexpected dollars in hand, Alice thanked them profusely and assured them that anything that wasn't used would be put into the Christmas fund.

Upon Alice's departure, Dexter and Spencer commenced to putting the soft drinks into a large cooler and then filling it with ice. They parked themselves in front of the television to watch football, but that didn't last long. Spencer was soon summoned for a last-minute trip to the store. He asked Dexter to come along, but Dexter declined in favor of helping Christina carry food over from next door.

"We can both help when we get back," Spencer suggested.

"Let me just check and see where she is with everything," Dexter replied, his thumbs already tapping out a text message to his beloved.

Spencer observed with a smirk. "When did you get so wrapped?" he teased.

"Just being a decent person, bro. I don't want to leave her hanging if she's ready to head over now." Dexter's phone buzzed with Christina's reply just then.

He tapped out a response before lifting his head to face his brother. "We're good to go. She'll be ready in about thirty minutes. I told her we'd stop by when we get back."

"We can just load everything up in the car then," Spencer said, starting the ignition.

"What are we getting at the store anyway?"

"Brown sugar and whipped topping," Spencer answered, adding, "and Paula will probably text me with another request before it's all said and done... hopefully *before* I'm in the checkout line."

"I'll see if Christina needs anything," Dexter said, busy with his phone.

Spencer regarded his baby brother. "She's really got you hooked, doesn't she?"

Dexter looked up, meeting his brother's eyes briefly. Spencer returned his gaze to the road out of necessity, but stole a glance when Dexter didn't respond right away. He had an unreadable expression on his face. Dexter wrestled with a response, ultimately deciding not to shy away from the teasing. He was blessed to have found love again and was not going to be timid about it just because Spencer (and Blair) liked to give him a hard time.

"I *am* hooked," he stated with a smile.

Spencer didn't say anything else for a moment. They arrived at the store. Since Christina hadn't needed anything, Dexter waited in the vehicle. When Spencer returned and they pulled back onto the road, he glanced over at Dexter and asked, "So, where is this heading?"

"This...?"

"This thing with you and Christina," Spencer clarified.

"I'm in love with her, and she's in love with me. I've been praying about it -- pretty sure I'm going to ask her to marry me."

Spencer blew out a breath of air and looked over at his brother. "Are you sure you want to jump back into *that* skillet?"

"I didn't think I'd ever go there willingly after the way things went down with Sarah, but the thought of not having Christina in my life is scarier than the thought of marriage."

"Well, she *is* a very attractive woman," Spencer replied.

Dexter cast a hard look in his brother's direction. "I don't disagree with that, but her beauty is only a fraction of the package."

"Oh, I don't doubt that."

Something about Spencer's tone made Dexter bristle, but he refrained from saying anything. They were nearly home, and he preferred not to get into a squabble on a holiday. As they pulled into Christina's driveway, Dexter admonished Spencer not to say anything about his intention to propose. "I want it to be a surprise," he said, "done just right and at the right time."
Spencer nodded his agreement and the brothers left the vehicle.

"Everything that needs to go is on the table," Christina indicated as she retrieved an ice box cake and a cranberry salad from the refrigerator. She carried them out as the Billings brothers carried out pies, casseroles, and the like. When they had finished, Spencer leaned against his vehicle as Dexter queried, "Are we forgetting anything?"

"I don't think so," Christina answered. "If we are, I'll bring it when I come."

"No lemonade?" Dexter asked, not bothering to hide the pouty disappointment.

"The lemonade! It's in the fridge downstairs."

"I'll just run and get it," offered Dexter, and without waiting for her agreement, he sprinted into the house.

Christina found herself alone with Spencer. She laughed nervously. "There's more room downstairs, but you know… out of sight is out of mind."

"Not always," he said without elaboration, his eyes considering her in a manner that made her long to escape. She didn't know what he meant by that, but she didn't really want to.

"I'm going to finish up," she said, turning back toward the house. Over her shoulder, she called, "I'll walk over in just a few minutes."

Dexter was coming out the door as she stepped onto the porch. He carried the large glass jar of lemonade in one arm and balanced a tray of deviled eggs with the other. "Do these go too?" he asked, tossing his head in the direction of the tray.

"Yep. Forgot about those too," she said with a grin. Christina tiptoed to grace Dexter's cheek with a kiss. "I'll be on over in a few minutes. Just got to wash up a couple of pans and change clothes. The kids should be there soon too."

"I'll see you in a bit then."

When Christina walked across the adjoining side yards twenty minutes later, she discovered that Haley and Jared had already arrived. Jordan's car was in the driveway too, so he and Briana must be here as well. Jared was nowhere to be seen, but Haley was sitting on the retaining wall talking to Dexter. *Odd.* "Hey, Mom," Haley greeted. "Jared helped carry some food in. We'll be in in a minute."

And with that, Christina was summarily dismissed. She didn't know what to make of it, but before she had time to give it much thought, Brianna opened the door. "Christina, thank God you're here! I think I've ruined the oriental slaw."

"What happened?"

"The recipe you gave me said to mix the dressing in right before serving, but I put it in when I was making it. I missed that part and didn't know I was supposed to wait."

"Let's have a look at it," Christina said. "I'm sure it'll be fine -- maybe just not as crunchy."

As they stepped across the threshold, Haley hollered for Briana to "send Jordan out here for a minute." Christina glanced back in time to see Haley flash an elated grin at Dexter. *Now, what are they up to?* Whatever it is, Jordan's about to be involved. *A Christmas present for someone, I bet.* Christina liked surprises, so she wouldn't pry.

Before Dexter made his way in, he had conferred with all three of Christina's children, Payton having arrived with Lily moments after Christina went inside. Haley's wedding plans were all in place and it was shaping up to be a very joyous holiday season!

Chapter Fourteen

Dexter groaned with a delicious misery, letting out the footrest to recline on one end of Christina's couch. "I've never seen so much food in my life!"

Christina, who sat on the other end with her feet tucked up to the side of her bottom, giggled. "It was quite a spread," she agreed, adding, "but you didn't have to sample *everything* just because it was there!"

"Sure I did!" he fired back. "I take my responsibilities very seriously. I don't like there being foods out there that I've never tried."

"You've had pumpkin pie before. You've had sweet potato casserole before."

"Well, I have to eat my favorites, don't I?" he quipped.

Christina laughed. "I ate too much too. We were certainly blessed with plenty."

Dexter nodded his agreement. A moment passed in comfortable silence before he commented, "I loved going around the room and naming what we were most thankful for."

"And *I* loved making your list," she said with a smile. He returned the smile, but said nothing. How could he even put into words how thankful he was for their love? How he counted her among God's best blessings? Christina went on, "We've always gone around the table at Thanksgiving and done kind of a chain prayer, each person thanking God specifically for their blessings and the last one asking His blessing on the meal. We couldn't do that with such a large group, of course, or we'd have never gotten to eat!"

"But it was the perfect topic of conversation while we ate. I'm so glad Payton mentioned it."

"So am I."

"Where *is* Payton?"

"He and Lily spent an hour or so serving dinner at the outreach center and then went to Lily's for another meal," Christina replied.

Dexter was impressed. The entire Sinclair family seemed to have a heart for others. He felt like a better man just by association! "He's an amazing young man," Dexter observed.

"He really is," she agreed with a thoughtful smile. "I don't know many people his age who can see the big picture. Most are so self-centered, but Payton doesn't forget to give back and to share his faith. When I was that age, serving at an outreach was the last thing on my mind. I was perfectly outraged over having to help with the dishes!"

Dexter chuckled. "That's a relief!" he said before he could censor himself.

"What do you mean?" she asked.

Great. Now he was going to have to explain. He looked at Christina, his mirth fading into a sincere smile as he debated how to express what was on his mind. "This is going to sound cheesy," he warned. She urged him on with eyes crinkled by a smile. "You put me to shame, Christina. I've always thought of myself as a good person -- willing to help others, chivalrous, follower of the golden rule. But you -- and every one of your children -- take that about a hundred steps further. It's a little intimidating!"

"Oh, Dexter," Christina said dismissively, obviously uncomfortable with this level of praise.

"I'm serious," he said, though his face was a mixture of...what? Teasing, sincerity, wistfulness? "It's a relief to know you're not so perfect, that you're on a journey just like the rest of us."

Christina sighed. "Apparently, I've been faking perfection a little too well. That can be dangerous," she quipped. "It's a long fall off a pedestal." Dexter laughed, but said nothing. She went on. "I'm so far from perfect that it's laughable, Dex. It's definitely a journey, and I may have come a long way, but I have a long way to go. So do my kids. So do most of us. Surely through all the mess with Becca and Gail, you've seen my flaws.

She paused as Dexter reflected on the trials Christina had experienced with her two best friends after Anthony had died. They and their husbands had spent lots of time --vacations, even -- with the Sinclairs. They took annual trips, had cookouts on a regular basis, and had established many traditions together. After Anthony passed, Becca and Gail were present and supportive at first, but then seemed to move on without Christina. Eventually, they seemed to have effectively *replaced* the Sinclairs with another couple. She was devastated. She was still grieving the loss of her husband, and kind of lost her closest friends too. But...

"I don't understand," he said, puzzled. "How were *you* at fault there? What flaws are you talking about?"

"That wasn't my finest hour," Christina said with a weak smile. "And truthfully, I still have my moments. I miss them *so* much, and though we're civil to one another and I'd do anything for them if they needed me, I know things will never be the same again. While I was wallowing in self-pity, I should have realized that God was in control. I should have recognized that He was placing people along the way to fill the void. But I didn't for a long time. I questioned Him and was even angry at Him for taking so much from me! How's that for flawed?"

"I was there for most of it, Christina. What I remember is you being human, that's all. I remember you giving voice to your trust in God's plan even as your heart was struggling to accept it, to own it. I know that none of us are technically perfect, but when I talk about you seeming that way, I mean that I see you praising God through the storms and putting others before yourself. And I won't lie -- I know I don't measure up. But I'm a better man when I'm around you, and being around you makes me *want* to be a better man."

Christina had inched closer to him as he spoke and now laid her head on his right shoulder as he instinctively lifted his arm to put around her. "Oh, Dex," she said, "I see all those same qualities in you and can't believe you don't see them in yourself!"

He gave her a one-armed squeeze. "I'll take your word for it," he said.

"Promise not to be too disappointed when my flaws make an appearance? I have plenty, you know."

"I'll try not to be," Dexter said with mock resignation. "What kind of flaws are we talking about here?"

"Well.... I can go a little overboard when I have new ideas," Christina ventured.

"Like with the mission work?"

"Yeah."

"That could easily be considered an attribute. Look what that zeal accomplished! Try again."

"I hate grocery shopping and only go when I have to. Even then, I never come in the front door. How ridiculous is that?"

Dexter knew that Christina had discovered Anthony in the living room after returning home from grocery shopping that day. Paula had discreetly put away the groceries after returning from the hospital. "Not ridiculous at all. You're proving *my* case, not *yours*!"

"Okay, smartypants... let's hear some of your flaws!" Christina demanded playfully.

"Well... I might snore just a little," he offered.

Christina gave a little pshaw sound and said, "That's nothing. Try again."

"I lose confidence in myself pretty easily," he admitted. "I question myself, blame myself when things go wrong...like with my marriage."

"I think we all have to self-examine when things don't go as planned. I'd much rather you be that way than be someone who never admits if they're wrong. So...not a valid flaw."

"Wow! We must both really be perfect then!" he laughed. "Good thing we found each other!"

"Yes," Christina agreed, "a very good thing." She rested her head contentedly against his shoulder, draping an arm over his chest. Dexter held her to him, relishing the unassuming intimacy of the moment. He ran his hand up and down her arm as she lay against him. It felt so good to just *be* here with her. It wasn't long before he felt the weight of her slight frame deepen, molding itself into his own contours. Noting the slow, rhythmic manner that her breathing had taken on, Dexter realized she had fallen asleep. He knew she must be exhausted! She had been cooking for two days!

He leaned his head back against the couch and closed his eyes. The full stomach (including a healthy dose of tryptophan from the turkey) and utter contentment of having Christina in his arms brought a drowsiness that he saw no need to fight. It would have been futile to fight it anyway. His last thought before sleep pulled him under was that it was such a rare treat to *sleep* with her. He so looked forward to the time that this would be a routine occurrence that they'd both take for granted. *Soon.*

Both Dexter and Christina were asleep when Payton got home. Dexter awoke to the quiet click of the shutter on Payton's phone camera. "What are you doing?" Dexter asked, half addled with sleep.

"Just sending a Snapchat to Haley. Well, and Jordan, Brianna, Jared, and Lily. Y'all are too cute."

Christina mumbled something that was muffled between Dexter's shirt and her hair that had fallen across her face. Dexter was amused. "What was that, hon?"

She lifted her head and pushed her hair back. "I said to send it to me too."

Payton chuckled, "Okay."

"You have Snapchat?" Dexter asked.

"I do," she answered.

"Since when?"

"I don't know. A year or so, I guess."

"I feel so out of the loop. Should I get it too?"

"You should," Christina said. "We'd have fun with it. And I'm only in the loop because my kids keep me there."

"Okay," Dexter said through a massive yawn. "Maybe tomorrow."

"Yeah, definitely not tonight," she said, adding, "I'm way too tired to teach you something new tonight."

Dexter stood, slipping on his shoes and retrieving his keys from the hook near the door. Christina turned her attention to Payton. "Did you and Lily have a nice time?"

"We did. I'm stuffed!"

Dexter chimed in, "I can't even imagine going to another dinner! I'm stuffed from just ours!"

Christina, who had joined him near the door, elbowed him lightly in the ribs. "Well, we *did* graze all evening!"

He laughed. "True enough."

Dexter bade Payton good night and hugged Christina tightly before stepping out onto the porch. He leaned back in to kiss her lips lightly. "It's been a wonderful Thanksgiving," he said. She nodded in agreement, stifling a yawn. "Go to bed, sweetie."

"That's my plan," she said with a sleepy smile. "I love you, Dex."

"I love you, too."

When he texted her twenty minutes later, there was no reply -- but he didn't know that until the next morning. Like Christina, he was asleep the instant his head hit the pillow.

~~~~~~~~~~

"So...no Black Friday shopping?" Blair asked when Dexter answered the phone the morning after Thanksgiving. Her initial question as to what he was doing had placed him at home reading. "Isn't that mandatory when you're in a relationship with a woman?"

Dexter laughed. "Not with Christina. She may catch a deal online for some random gifts, but her family doesn't do Christmas the way everyone else does."

"I know Christmas involves mission work and all...don't they buy for one another?"

"They give each other one meaningful gift, but since Anthony died, Christina says they've worked really hard as a family to keep the focus on the true meaning of Christmas."

"That's really phenomenal," Blair said. "It's not easy to tear away from the commercialism and societal pressures."

"Yeah, it's really something," Dexter agreed. "*She's* really something."

"That's kinda the reason I called. I just wanted to tell you that the more I'm around Christina, the more I like her. I'm glad she's in your life."

"I'm glad too, sis."

"It's good to see you happy."

Dexter smiled, silently acknowledging that he *was* happy -- happier than he could have ever imagined. And hopefully it was only the beginning. "Hey, you'll be at Haley and Jared's wedding, right?"

"Probably," she replied. "I mean, I plan to if nothing comes up."

"No, I need you to be there," Dexter said with a good bit of urgency. "Make it a priority, okay?"

"Um...okay. Since when are you so into weddings?"

"Just be there. You won't want to miss this one."

"I thought it was just supposed to be a smallish affair."

"It is," he confirmed. "Just an intimate gathering, but it's important for you and Spencer and Paula to be there."

Blair mulled that over for a moment, debating whether to press him about this new development. Her brother had never been much on ceremony before, and she didn't know what to make of his insistence that she attend this one. She chalked it up to his trying to impress his gal. Blair decided on a different tact. "Can I bring a 'plus one'?"

Dexter was completely caught off guard on the other end of the line. Was Blair dating someone? "Well, yeah," he said. When she didn't respond right away, he asked, "Is there something I should know?"

Blair laughed. "There's nothing to tell...yet. But I promise, you'll be the first to know."

He told his little sister that he was holding her to that, and the call ended after a brief exchange of small talk (which centered primarily around the array of food at the previous day's dinner). Dexter wasn't much on black Friday shopping, but he had one *meaningful* gift to pick out for Christina. As loath as he was to face the crowds of shoppers, he was suddenly very eager to make his selection. The afternoon found him, not at a mall, but strolling the streets of his hometown in search of the perfect gift for the love of his life.

~~~~~~~~~~

November relinquished its grip and passed the torch to December. As if by mutual agreement, November took the last of the bountiful harvest, pumpkins, and chrysanthemums while December ushered in the spirit of Christmas, adorned with twinkling lights and scented with gingerbread and pine. In the week that followed Thanksgiving, the whole world was transformed into something magical and almost sacred. Christmas carols played from every speaker. Church services became more reverent as the glad tidings were retold and the nativity reenacted.

Dexter ignored as many of the commercials as he could and strove to follow Christina's lead by keeping the focus on Christ, God's gift to the world. His emphasis was on acts of kindness rather than material gifts.

Haley's wedding was scheduled for December 23rd, a twilight ceremony in Christina's home church. It was fast approaching. Haley had only two weeks of classes left in the semester. After the wedding, Jared planned to take her on honeymoon for a week in some tropical location. As for the rest of the family, including Dexter, their Christmas destination was the children's hospital. They would spend a week there being "the hands and feet of Christ," as Christina liked to say. Dexter was excited about the entire month of December. It was an exhilarating time for the Sinclair family, and hopefully the Billings family too.

Chapter Fifteen

The hanging of the greens normally yielded a singular magnificent tree in the corner of the sanctuary to the right of the pulpit with a poinsettia here and there and a festive wreath on the front door of the church. He had visited the church where Christina was a member during the Christmas season before. The scene Dexter beheld this evening, however, made the usual church decorations look like a Charlie Brown Christmas! The funny thing was that he was present, helping when the trees were erected and the lights were strung. He had been at the church all day, in fact, working alongside Christina as she decorated for the momentous event. The magic had been in the finishing touches, apparently... in the sparkling lights and the dozens of poinsettias, the exquisite dove ornaments and the sheer, dreamy bows. It was a veritable wonderland!

It seemed that all of this had happened in the two hours since he had left to get cleaned up and fetch a half dozen bags of ice for the reception. The reception... he wondered about the transformation in the fellowship hall. If it was anything like that of the sanctuary, everything about this event was going to be absolutely enchanting. He sat on the second pew from the front, where Christina would join him after she was escorted in. As Dexter waited, he marveled at this display of love. Haley was very laid back, easygoing... she hadn't been very particular about the details of the wedding planning. According to Christina, Haley had brushed off the need for decoration at all, indicating that the church would already be decorated for Christmas anyway. The latest text message from Christina revealed that Haley had been ushered in through the backdoor to finish getting ready. She had not seen the enhanced adornment of the church. This was Christina's gift to her daughter.

As he sat there, soft instrumental melodies began to play. Tender refrains of *It Came Upon a Midnight Clear*, *O Holy Night,* and *O Little Town of Bethlehem* piped through the speakers as guests were seated. He turned around occasionally to witness the modest crowd assemble and happened to spy Blair being seated a few rows back. A young man sat down next to her, and they were soon joined by Paula and Spencer. *Well, I'll be!* he thought. *She* did *bring a date!*

Soon, Christina was ushered in and seated next to him. His first glimpse of her robbed him of the ability to breathe properly. Dexter actually had to *instruct* his lungs to pull in air. "You look stunning," he whispered.

Christina accepted the compliment and a kiss on the cheek. "You look pretty amazing yourself."

"I showered," he said with a grin. "I hoped you'd notice."

The music paused and then resumed at a slightly increased volume. It sounded like harps. *Silent Night* provided a charming backdrop as the pastor and the bridal party entered. Jared waited serenely at the front of the church. *Silent Night* faded and *The Wedding March* began to play. The entire audience rose and turned to watch as Jordan escorted his little sister in. Haley glanced over at her mother with misty eyes and mouthed *thank you.* On behalf of the family, Jordan gave Haley to be married and then sat down next to Brianna.

Pastor Lawrence began the ceremony that celebrated the birth of Jesus and compared the institution of marriage to Jesus' relationship to His church. His message was simple and concise -- just perfect. Haley and Jared exchanged vows and rings and before he knew what was what, they were pronounced husband and wife. Christina held up remarkably well next to him, only dabbing her eyes occasionally.

A receiving line was formed down the corridor leading to the fellowship hall. Christina pulled him along as she went to stand next to her daughter, which delighted Dexter. After greeting all the guests and shaking countless hands, he was kindly released to keep an eye on the reception as Christina, the families, and the wedding party lingered for a few photographs. The fellowship hall did not disappoint, the transformation exceeding his expectations. There were two clusters of three trees on either side of the table where Haley and Jared would sit. Each tree was adorned with realistic looking doves and the same beautiful ribbon as had been used in the sanctuary.

The tables were covered with white tablecloths and adorned with pine cones and small trees. The table that held the three tiered white cake, the one that held a healthy stack of gifts, and the one designated for the bride and groom all sported a tasteful silver table runner and were accented with lush poinsettias. A punch comprised of ginger ale and some kind of nearly clear fruit juice flowed from a fountain into a pool in which cranberries floated. Dexter looked around and marvelled at how everything could be so simple and so spectacular at the same time. Christina had outdone herself, he thought… it was all lovely.

Dexter walked over to the table where Spencer and Paula sat. With no sign of his sister, he asked, "Blair didn't leave, did she?"

"She's in the restroom," Paula answered.

"You met her friend." It was more a statement than a question.

"He seems very nice," Paula assured him.

"Here they come," Spencer pointed out.

Dexter stood to greet Blair. He extended a hand in the direction of her companion, who Blair introduced as Rob. A good firm handshake was reassuring.

"It's nice to meet you, Rob."

"Likewise," said Rob.

They sat, filling the wait with small talk. Soft Christmas music began to play from the speakers and the guests chatted amicably. It wasn't long before the bridal party and their families entered the fellowship hall. Again, Haley's delight was written on her face.

Haley and Jared took a seat at their special table, and Dexter got up to join Christina at a table near the front. They were accompanied by Jordan, Brianna, Payton, and Lily. The traditional wedding reception activities commenced with a change in music. There were dances, toasts, cake, and well-wishes until finally it was time to toss the bouquet and fling the garter.

All the single ladies, put your hands up piped through the speakers and brought everyone to attention. A formation of all the young singles was already forming by the time the announcement was made.

"Go on, Mom," Payton said.

"Me?!" Christina said, as if it hadn't dawned on her that she was technically eligible for participation.

"Yeah, *you*!" Lily laughed, pulling her into the circle of single women. "Come with me. Maybe one of us will get lucky!"

Christina laughed and let herself be dragged onto the floor. Dexter got up with a chuckle and walked toward a spot with a better view. As he passed his family's table, he heard Spencer mutter something to the rest of the table about Dexter getting nervous that Christina might catch the bouquet. Dexter only smirked, knowing that this wouldn't bother him in the least. He found an opening in the crowd near where Lily had led Christina. Lily flashed him a smile when their eyes met, but Christina didn't notice that he had moved.

Lots of chatter and mirth held the moment out. Finally, Haley took her position with her back to the crowd of waiting single women. She glanced back over her shoulder, sweeping a smile at her friends, her mother, and her brother's girlfriend. She turned back around and held the bouquet out in front of her. She made a movement as if to fling the bouquet over her head, effectively faking everyone out. A collective groan rose from the crowd, followed by good-natured laughter. She glanced back, caught Dexter's eye, and winked. Haley held the bouquet out once more, directly in front of her with stiff arms. She took a deep breath, savoring the suspense, and then -- in one swift move -- pivoted, raised and lowered her arms, and took three steps to stand directly in front of her mother. The bouquet was extended between them. Christina looked down at it, and back up at Haley, slack-jawed and confused.

Haley gave the bouquet a gentle thrust, forcing Christina to take it from her just as Dexter slid onto bended knee from her right. Leaving the bouquet in her mother's hand, Haley stepped back as her brothers stepped forward on either side. The entire audience was silent as they watched the scene unfold.

Dexter opened a small black box to reveal the *perfect gift* he had found for the love of his life. He extended it toward Christina and raised his glistening eyes to meet hers. Christina gasped, covering her mouth with a shaking hand. A tear spilled involuntarily onto her cheek. Lily stepped in quietly and took the bouquet from Christina, freeing her hand for Dexter to grasp. He pulled the ring free from its box and held it up for Christina to behold.

"Christina," he said breathily, "The Bible says that God can bring good from bad. I believe His hand has been on what we've found together. After all that we've both been through, I believe that He has allowed some good to come into our lives. He allowed *us* to come into *each other's* lives. I never thought I'd be brave enough to love someone again, but I was wrong. I love you with all my heart. And if you'll have me, I promise to love you for the rest of my life. He paused, swallowing hard. Christina twisted around, seeking out her children. The three of them huddled together. Her eyes posed the unspoken question that they eagerly answered -- all three of them -- with subtle, but unmistakable nods. She turned her attention back to the man she loved, who was yet on bended knee before her.

"Christina Sinclair," he said, poising the diamond ring just beyond the tip of the appropriate finger, "Will you marry me?"

He held his breath, his eyes never leaving hers. A slow smile spread across Christina's face. Tears moistened her cheeks. She was nodding. *This was good!* "Yes," she finally managed when her voice caught up with her mind, her heart.

Dexter slipped the ring down onto her finger and Christina repeated, "Yes," this time more strongly. He rose quickly. She let out a squeal as he took her into his arms. Dexter whirled her around and kissed her soundly. When he let her go, the crowd closed in to offer congratulations. Christina's children were first in line; they held her in a long embrace, followed by Brianna, Lily, and Jared. Meanwhile, Spencer, Paula, and Blair encased Dexter in a tangle of well-wishing arms. When Haley moved in to hug Dexter, she whispered conspiratorially, "We pulled *that* off beautifully!"

Dexter smiled broadly. "I don't think she saw it coming at all. Thanks for sharing your spotlight."

Haley pulled back from the embrace, meeting his gaze. "It was *truly* my pleasure. I wish you and Mom every happiness. Congratulations."

"Let's not forget who the bride is here," Dexter said with a laugh. "Congratulations to you and Jared!"

Haley thanked him and stepped out of the way. Others were waiting to convey their best wishes. When things settled down, they went through the motions of tossing the garter. The bouquet incident had taken the wind out of that sail though, and Jared pretty much just tossed it to Dexter. It was fitting, and everyone just laughed. And then guests began to leave. Haley and Jared departed for their honeymoon.

Pastor Lawrence's wife, Melissa, who had become a close friend of Christina's, stayed behind to help disassemble trees and take down decorations. Paula stayed as well, as did Christina's boys and their ladies. Between the lot of them, they had the church restored to its usual state within a couple of hours. Dexter was exhausted! He could only imagine how tired Christina was!

"Are you sure we have to get up early in the morning for the children's hospital?" he asked his new fiance with a teasing smile.

"How about we leave at 9:00 instead of 7:00?" Christina replied, stifling a yawn.

"Hey, marriage is going to be a piece of cake if you're always so quick to compromise!"

"I'm very easy to get along with. You made a good decision," she quipped.

Dexter laughed and drew her into his arms. "You've made me a very happy man," he said, holding her close to him. "You've also made me a very tired man."

Christina playfully swatted his shoulder, drawing back. She held her left hand up to admire the ring. "The kids knew…"

Dexter nodded. "They were all in on it. I had to have their blessing, of course, and Haley was a doll about the whole thing."

"I can't believe it! I'm going to be Christina Billings!"

"I like the sound of that!" he said, and then, "Everyone was so happy for us, weren't they?"

Christina nodded vigorously. "Melissa has the whole thing recorded. She said it was the sweetest thing she had ever seen."

Dexter brushed his fingernail on his lapel and then held them out, making a show of inspecting them. "Well, you know… I'm a romantic guy." They shared a laugh and then Dexter sobered. "Speaking of everyone being happy for us, I know I saw Gail and Becca at the wedding. Did neither of them stay for the reception?"

"I don't think so." Christina's tone had fallen flat. The strained friendships remained a tender spot.

Dexter didn't want to compromise the joy of their day. "We had a much bigger crowd than I was expecting though," he offered. "They were all so sincere in their wishes for our happiness."

"Yes, it was heartwarming," Christina agreed, rallying.

The two of them lingered in the foyer, reluctant to part, but undeniably tired. Soon, Dexter realized, they would be heading home *together*. They had a lot of decisions to make about how and when to make that happen, but those were conversations for another day. This day could be put to bed with the assurance that Christina would soon be his wife. And that was enough for today.

Chapter Sixteen

The four days spent at the children's hospital were the most grueling, humbling, and altogether gratifying of Dexter's life thus far. He had helped out with different aspects of the mission efforts over the months, and had even accompanied Christina to the hospital before. But there was just something about being in that place, surrounded by those life and death circumstances through Christmas that was profoundly moving.

Parents were torn between maintaining some sense of normalcy for their families, their sick children as well as their healthy children, and wading through the dark reality that included needle sticks, emesis basins, and oxygen tubes. Sweet young faces whose greatest concern should have been staying on Santa's "nice" list instead told a tale of uncertainty and fear. The joy of the season was overshadowed by test results and clinical trials.

The staff, aided by the Anthony Sinclair Mission Foundation, made a valiant effort to turn that around. Throughout the month of December, there were Christmas decorations adorning the rooms and corridors. But through the coordinated efforts of the foundation and local volunteers, Christmas Eve brought dozens of *elves* with dozens of trees and hundreds of gifts. Dexter was astounded. *How?* When he gave voice to his question, Christina explained that local volunteers had compiled a list of nearby stores, which Christina and others had contacted. Many of them agreed to donate imperfect trees that had been returned, minimally damaged ornaments, and other decorations. Some stores had even provided employees to come and help set up and decorate the trees. The ASMF purchased elf and Santa hats in bulk, providing them to all the helpers. In a matter of hours, the place had been transformed. And for just a little while, the sickness and worry took a backseat to the magic of Christmas.

"And what about all the gifts?" Dexter asked.

"Donations from all our partners."

"Wow! I had no idea that the foundation was so well established now that all this work was being carried out whether you're here or not."

"I've found that most people want to help, but just don't know how. When we tell them specifically what is needed... well, they make it happen."

"How can I be most useful?" Dexter asked, looking around at the bustle of activity. Everyone seemed to know what to do.

"Oh, just jump in anywhere you see a need," Christina said, adding, "You might check and see if there's more stuff to carry in and, if not, check patient rooms to see if trees are up and lights working, etc."

"Okay,"

"You know how it goes, Dex. The Lord will show you the needs. If you see a kid that needs to talk or a parent that needs a break, forget about the trees. They'll get put up."

"Right," he said, offering a smile.

Dexter walked down the corridor, peeking into occasional rooms uncertainly. Nothing grabbed his attention, and he didn't see any trees in the patients' rooms. Soon he met up with a young man with a Christmas tree box hoisted onto one shoulder. He lingered at the doorway of the room where the young man deposited the tree. An older woman was standing near the window. She turned around to smile a greeting, but said nothing. "I'm here to help," Dexter told the guy. "Are there more boxes to carry in?"

The man extended his hand. "Mike."

"Dexter."

Mike pulled an elf hat from his pocket and handed it to Dexter. "Merry Christmas, man."

Dexter took the hat, placing it on his head without hesitation. "Thanks," he said with a grin.

"We've kind of got the hauling under control," Mike said. "How 'bout getting started with the trees?" He tilted his head in the direction of the one he had just put down.

"I can do it."

"Great," Mike said, disappearing through the doorway and humming *Little Drummer Boy* as he proceeded down the hallway.

Dexter turned to the woman who had witnessed the exchange, but had yet to say anything. He offered a smile, which was returned. "I'm Ruth," she said.

He crossed the room and shook hands with Ruth. "Pleased to meet you. I'm Dexter."

"Dexter, what's the best thing that's happened to you today?"

She surprised him with such a random question. A nervous chuckle escaped him and he scratched his head. "Well, um..." He looked up at her and grinned. "I woke up an engaged man this morning," he offered.

Ruth's eyes twinkled. "Is that so?!" she exclaimed with delight.

"Yes," Dexter confirmed, and the older woman insisted that he tell her all about it. The two of them began to mindlessly unbox the tree and assemble it while they talked. After sharing his story about the engagement,

Dexter asked, "The patient in this room... it's a family member?"

"My grandson," she said. "His name is Titus. He's ten, diagnosed with leukemia at age seven. It's been a long road, but the best thing that's happened to me today? His latest lab work showed improvement."

"That's great! Does that mean he's going to be okay?"

"Only God knows the answer to that question. But it *does* mean we can all be together for Christmas -- even if it *is* here -- without having to wear masks."

"Well, that's... something," Dexter offered hesitantly.

"It is indeed, and we take whatever tidbits of good news we can get." She smiled at him kindly.

Just then, a pale boy who must have been Titus appeared. He was in a wheelchair that was pushed by a guy in scrubs. "Woah, a Christmas tree! Is that staying in here?" His enthusiasm was immediate and almost comical.

Ruth glanced at Dexter, her eyes bright. "I think so."

"That's the plan!" Dexter confirmed, knowing that he would have gone out and bought a tree himself in order to avoid the disappointment that would surely come with a negative answer. "I've heard rumors of stockings being hung too," he added conspiratorially.

"Cool!" Titus exclaimed. He crinkled up his nose. "Who *are* you?"

"My name is Dexter." Dexter pointed to his hat. "I'm an elf that's been sent here to bring a little Christmas magic."

Titus gave him a dubious look. He was probably a little too old to buy into the whole North Pole thing, but Dexter watched as the boy made the decision to go along with it. "I saw others in the hall, but didn't know I'd find my very own elf in my room!" Dexter chuckled. Titus asked, "Can I put whatever I want on the tree?"

"Within reason," Ruth interjected. "Santa and all his elves are busy! They're trying to bring Christmas to everyone."

Titus looked at his grandmother, and then back to Dexter. "One time at school we painted popsicle sticks to look like snowmen. Maybe we could get some mouth sticks and make some ornaments."

"Tongue depressors?" Dexter guessed. Titus nodded his head. "I bet we *could* find some of those around here! Just out of curiosity though, if you could have anything you wanted to decorate your tree, what would it be?"

"Star Wars ornaments!" Titus answered without hesitation. "My dad loves Star Wars. We watch the movies all the time. He says I'm his little Jedi!"

"Do you have all the movies?"

Ruth chuckled. "He has movies and action figures and all kinds of stuff."

Dexter smiled at Ruth and then turned back to Titus. "That's awesome!"

"Maybe we could paint some of those tongue depressors to look like characters," Ruth offered. "CP3O would be easy enough."

"Oh, Nana, I bet we could!" Dexter loved how Titus could latch onto anything and get excited about it.

"Your mom will be back in a little while. We'll have her to find some ideas on her phone... on that Pinterest."

"Meanwhile, what kind of lights do you want? Clear or colors?" Dexter asked.

"Woah, you mean I get to pick?!"

"Yep!"

"Colors," Titus declared. "Mom never lets us have colors at home."

"I'm going to see what I can find," Dexter said, stepping toward the doorway. "Do you think you could help your nana finish fluffing out the tree?"

"Sure," Titus said agreeably.

Dexter went in search of colored lights and Star Wars ornaments. He found the lights, easily enough. A good variety had been donated. All the ornaments were typical fare though... no Star Wars. He touched base with Christina, who put someone on the task of locating a store that carried such ornaments. "This is the kind of thing I was talking about," Christina said excitedly. "These kiddos, these families need someone who cares enough to get personal and make an impact. Ornaments seem like such a small thing, but you have no idea how much of a difference you might be making to this family!"

He grinned, relieved. It seemed so trivial in the big scheme of things, and he was afraid she would think he was getting hung up on something that wasn't worthy of so much attention. Dexter had bumped into Christina near the nurses' station, but had no idea how she had spent the past hour or so. "What have you been up to while I've been with Titus and Ruth?"

"I always head straight to the nursery," she said with a smile. "I've been rocking babies."

Dexter gave her a smile that faltered. "What is it?" she asked, reading a struggle on his face.

"Honestly?" She nodded, urging him on. He continued, "I think you and I have both done a beautiful job of coming to terms with our pasts and the fact that each other has a history. We're just happy to have today and a future to look forward to. But I'm never more jealous of Anthony than when I think about him getting *that* season with you -- the season of rocking babies."

"Oh, Dex." Christina wrapped her arms around him and rested her head on his chest. "That season will loop back around when grandbabies start coming, and we'll get to experience that together."

"Grandbabies?" It wasn't something Dexter had thought about much.

"Yeah, I mean it's bound to happen at some point. Two of my kids are married now and the third probably won't be far behind. You know how it goes for the younger set -- first comes love, then comes marriage…"

"Well, not everyone gets to the baby carriage part," he said, flashing a bittersweet smile as they both acknowledged his childless state. He truly didn't regret not having children with Sarah, and had told Christina as much. But he would have happily raised a family with Christina. "But I guess you're right. We *are* likely to have little ones in the family. It's what generally happens next. And I can't wait to experience that with you." Anthony had the first round, and in his absence, Dexter would be honored to take the second round.

Christina's phone buzzed. She looked at the screen, and then at Dexter. "We have Star Wars ornaments," she said. "One of our elves found them at a toy and hobby store. They're making a run for them and will bring back anything interesting they can find... like Star Wars wrapping paper or something suitable for a tree topper. If you know of anything in particular he should look for, I can text him and have him look."

"Wow! That's awesome," Dexter said. "I don't even know what he has or what he's asking for."

"See what you can find out."

Dexter agreed and headed back to Titus' room. The little boy looked so frail lying there in bed. Ruth and another woman were nearby. Dexter guessed that the woman was Titus' mother. It looked like Ruth was leaving. With Titus not having noticed his presence yet, Dexter just lingered outside the door until Ruth came out. Her eyes lit up with recognition when she saw him.

"May I walk you out?" he asked.

"Of course," Ruth said, slipping an arm through his.

'Was that Titus' mother in the room?"

"Yes, my daughter-in-law, Lisa. Titus' daddy is my son, Jack."

"It must be hard juggling work and other responsibilities with hospital visits and all," Dexter remarked thoughtfully.

"Yes, it has been a challenge, but we divide and conquer. Someone is with Titus most of the time. When we aren't here, we're pitching in with Talia or whatever needs to be done."

"Talia is his sister?

"Yes, she's four. Bless her soul -- she doesn't remember a time when Titus wasn't sick."

The pair stepped into the elevator. "How will Christmas be handled with Titus being here?"

"Jack and Lisa have debated about what to do. Titus has been sick off and on for quite a while, but this is the first year he has been hospitalized during Christmas. I think the plan is for Lisa to stay the night here. Jack is going to hang with Talia -- bake cookies and put them out for Santa, let her find her stocking in the morning, maybe facetime Titus and Lisa in the meantime for some *Twas the Night Before Christmas*."

"And gifts?"

"They're all going to be under Titus' tree. The four of them will open gifts here at the hospital in the morning."

"What does Titus want for Christmas?"

"He never asks for anything much. He likes to draw and read.... And anything related to Star Wars, of course. But he's not a kid that keeps a running list for Old Saint Nick."

"Sounds like he's easy to please and probably just wants to be well," Dexter said with a sigh.

"Yes," Ruth said, stepping out of the elevator, "that's what we *all* want. We would all give up material presents forever if we could just have him healthy." She pulled a wadded tissue from her sleeve and wiped her eyes.

Dexter reached for her hand and gave it a pat. "Ruth, may I pray with you before you leave?"

The older woman looked up at him so sharply that Dexter was afraid he had offended her. When her eyes warmed and fresh tears sprang forth, however, he realized that she was just surprised. She nodded her head. "I'd like that very much." The two of them stepped into an alcove, where Dexter beseeched the Lord for restoration of Titus' health and strength for the journey, for His blessing on the

154

efforts of everyone working to help the families in that hospital, for the stamina and determination of every person struggling to keep their focus on Him this season. Ruth echoed Dexter's amen and thanked him profusely. The two of them exchanged phone numbers, and Dexter promised to see her the next day.

Returning to Titus' room, Dexter bore multi-colored lights that brought a smile to the child's face. "I'm Dex," he said to Lisa.

She offered a hand, which he shook as she confirmed, "I'm Lisa, Ty's mom."

"He brought my tree!" Titus provided.

Dexter turned to him, holding up three boxes. "And now I'm bringing light. *And...* I have it on good authority that we have some special ornaments on the way."

"Cool! Can we go ahead and put the lights on?"

"Sure thing," Dexter answered.

"Look, Mom," Titus said, "They let me have colored lights!"

She cast an apologetic look toward Dexter, one that spoke volumes of the battles she would choose *not* to fight and small pleasures she would never deny if only she could have him healthy and at home. Dexter's eyes crinkled with a half-smile. "Hey, I never saw a Christmas light that wasn't beautiful. I like them all."

The special Star Wars ornaments were delivered by another "elf" just as they were finishing with the lights, much to Titus' delight. "Woah! This is awesome!" Dexter was even able to rig two light sabers into some semblance of a tree topper. Titus was positively beside himself and couldn't wait to show his dad, Talia, and Nana.

Dexter hung a stocking on a command hook near the tree and excused himself to other "elfish" duties. He looked at Lisa. "I understand Santa is delivering Christmas to the whole family here tonight." She confirmed, and Dexter scribbled on a piece of paper and handed it to her.

Lisa read his words: **Holler if you need help.** He included his phone number. She looked up with grateful eyes, and Dexter bade them a good night and a merry Christmas.

The call for help came hours later. Dexter had found Christina, persuaded her to leave the hospital for dinner, and filled her in on all the details about Titus and his family. Then he joined her in the nursery and assisted with feeding and comforting babies. Stockings hung on the end of every crib and a series of Christmas trees gently lit the expansive room. Christina looked exceptionally beautiful in the delicate light. He fell in love with her all over again as he watched her cradling a fragile two-month-old. She deftly maneuvered around tubes of all sorts to elicit a burp from the infant. Dexter was mesmerized as Christina hummed softly and patted the baby's back.

She had just laid the baby in its crib when Dexter felt his phone buzz. He pulled his phone from his pocket and looked at the screen. "It's Titus' mother. She needs a little help."

"Let's go!" Christina said, eager to meet the family.

Lisa stood and met Dexter and Christina at the door, stepping into the hallway as introductions were made. Dexter couldn't help but smile at how good it felt to introduce Christina as his fiancé. Christina suggested that stocking fillers be brought with the initial load so that she could work on that while she stayed with Titus. Dexter and Lisa retrieved two rolling carts from a nearby nurses' station, and began bringing in gifts. All over the entire hospital similar Santa business was being conducted. It was amazing to see!

Patients who were awake were whisked away for urgent faux tests. Stockings were stuffed and gifts were left beneath trees. Even the few unfortunate patients whose medical needs had frightened young parents away had full stockings and a few gifts upon awakening or returning. Dexter was surprised to see Santa himself making an appearance to add to the validity of their endeavors.

He and Christina ran on pure adrenaline, it seemed. When they reflected on how busy they had been during the past couple of weeks -- with the wedding and Christmas, and for Dexter, orchestrating a magnificent surprise engagement -- it was a wonder they were still standing. When they returned home the day after Christmas, Dexter fully expected to sleep until New Year's Eve! For now though, they would catch a power nap in an empty room before rising to spend Christmas day with the families of the children's hospital. And at 4 a.m., Dexter laid his head on an unfamiliar pillow and slept the gratifying sleep of the exhausted.

~~~~~~~~~~

Christina woke him gently at 7:20. "Merry Christmas, Dex" She planted a kiss on his unshaven face. Dexter couldn't think of a better way to be awakened. Christina had actually slept in the bed across the room, something they would have never considered under other circumstances...like a hotel room. But here, appearances didn't matter. The door was ajar. There was no privacy that could be counted on. And besides, they were both so utterly drained that they'd have done well to manage a good night kiss! *Had* they managed that much? Dexter had no idea.

Still it was a very intimate thing to sleep in the same room, and it warmed Dexter to know he had shared the night -- one he was apparently too exhausted to remember -- with Christina. He could hardly wait to spend *every* night with her. He hoped that when they finally had time to make plans, their marriage would be sooner rather than later.

Dexter sat up on the edge of the bed. "Good morning," he said through a sleepy grin. His voice was gravelly at first. "Merry Christmas to you too." Mindful of his morning breath, he was careful to press his lips to the side of Christina's face, not on her lips like he would have preferred.

"You've given me my gift already," Christina said, looking down at her ring, "now I have something for you."

"Are you kidding me? Your gift was putting that ring on. I don't need anything else."

"I knew you'd say that," she chuckled. "But I think you'll like this." Christina held out a fairly large box wrapped in solid red paper and sporting a festive white bow.

Dexter took the box. It wasn't heavy. He gave it a little shake and could both hear and feel the contents shifting within. He grinned at Christina.

"Open it," she urged.

He tore the paper, revealing the sturdy white box beneath it. Dexter opened the lid. Inside there were lots of smaller gifts, each wrapped in their own white paper. The one on top had black letters on it instructing him to "open now" and wishing him "Merry Christmas." He held it in his hand and with the other sifted through the assortment of boxes. Each of them had instructions. "Open when you're feeling insecure." "Open if you ever doubt my love." "Open when you've had a bad day." "Open on Valentine's Day." And so forth. There must be more than a dozen gifts inside the larger box. Maybe closer to *two* dozen!

"Oh my gosh, Christina!" She took the box from his lap and set it aside. He yet held the smaller parcel that asked to be opened immediately. Christina looked at him expectantly.

He opened it carefully, savoring the anticipation. When he got down to the box beneath the paper, Dexter looked up at Christina and grinned. She mirrored his smile and waited for him to lift the lid from the box. He pulled it open, revealing an elegant key ring -- the heavy kind that are often given as gifts. On the front, adhered to it was an abstract heart made of some unidentified substance. The heart was blurry in an artistic way that somehow conveyed a journey. Its message seemed to be that love had won out in the end, even if it hadn't been easy along the way. Dexter lifted the item from its velvet cradle, holding it in the palm of his hand. "I love it," he said, meaning it. How could he describe the message he perceived in that unusual heart? Did Christina get the same thing from it? Is that why she chose it?

Christina wordlessly turned the key ring over in Dexter's hand. Engraved on the back was *Romans 8:28.*

Just that -- not the actual verse. There was no need for that. This verse had come to mean so much to them that they could quote it without thought. More than once, they had marveled that the love they'd found together epitomized the promise in that verse. Tears misted Dexter's eyes and he leaned down, touching Christina's head with his own. In unison, they spoke that promise.

And we know that all things work together for good to them that love God, to them who are the called according to His purpose.

Chapter Seventeen

Dexter hugged Christina, thanking her for the gift, declaring that it was perfect. While he yet held her in his embrace, he turned his thanks to God. Tears streamed down his face as he thanked the Lord for bringing them together, asked His blessing on their day as well as their upcoming marriage and life together, and begged God for Titus' healing. He also asked for healing according to God's will for every sick child in that hospital.

He felt guilty that he beseeched God so passionately on Ty's behalf when he wanted them all to be well, but had treated the others as an afterthought. He said as much to Christina, embarrassed. She smiled knowingly. "Every time I'm here, there is one or two that I connect with -- and when I pray for them, it's personal. I think those connections are the reason God brought us here. I think Godly people are needed here, making connections and praying personal prayers for specific children. We want them *all* to be well, of course, and pray for that. But I tend to believe God is meeting the needs of each child in His own way. We connect with the ones He sends us to and through faith and obedience, we unlock His power with prayer. It's not possible to connect with all of them at that level, but I'd be willing to bet that God has someone else that He's using with the others."

Dexter was relieved at Christina's explanation. It made sense, and he embraced it. "I'd say you're right," he concurred. Christina's phone buzzed. She held it out so they could both read the screen. A photo of a bright-eyed baby with a message.

I have someone here who takes her medicine much better when you're around!

Christina grinned broadly and tapped out a response.

On my way!

She took five minutes to freshen up, grabbed a granola bar from her bag, and kissed Dexter. "Meet me in the dining hall around ten," she said. "We'll help with getting Christmas dinner ready to serve."

"Sounds good, babe," he said.

When Christina was gone, Dexter checked his phone. There was a message from Blair wishing him a Merry Christmas. He returned the greeting and then sent a similar message to Spencer and Paula. He used the bathroom and brushed his teeth, wondering about how Christmas morning was going for Titus and his family. He didn't want to intrude though, and figured he would see them at Christmas dinner. Meanwhile, his stomach was growling and he knew it would take more than one of Christina's granola bars to tide him over until then.

Twenty minutes later, Dexter was taking a bite of the breakfast sandwich that he'd ordered when he felt his phone buzz in his pocket. It was a text message from Ruth.

Merry Christmas! Ruth here. You may be busy, but Ty is asking for you.

That was all the encouragement Dexter needed. He wolfed down his sandwich and took his coffee with him. Only when he was in the elevator did he even take time to text Ruth back and say he was on his way. The blessed sound of laughter reached his ears before he reached Titus' room. Dexter stood hesitantly in the doorway. The room was quite a sight to behold! Much like the living rooms of homes all around the world, it was littered with crumpled wrapping paper and torn

162

boxes. And it was full of people. Ruth and Lisa, he knew. And Titus, of course. Lisa stood and ushered Dexter in. She introduced him to Titus' father, Jack, and his little sister, Talia. With a room full of loved ones, Dexter was touched that Titus had any interest in him being around.

But he did. The little guy's eyes lit up as soon as he saw Dexter. Talia was on the bed with her brother. They appeared to have been playing a game, but this was quickly abandoned in favor of showing off their new things. Both children were exuberant, but Dexter thought Titus looked a little tired.

"How long have you been up, buddy?" Dexter asked.

"It was early," he said, looking at Lisa. "Right, Mom?"

Lisa arched an eyebrow and supplied, "They came in to check his vitals at 5:00, and it was all over with once he saw all the presents!"

"But I couldn't open any of them," Titus said petulantly, "not until *they* got here." A general wave of his arm indicated his dad and sister.

"It's nice to have the whole family together when you're opening gifts," Dexter offered. "That's the way my family always did it."

"Yeah," Titus conceded. "And at least I got to check out my stocking. Talia's stocking was at home."

"Cool." Dexter ruffled the boy's head.

Dexter chatted with the family for a little while, enjoying their company. *Such good people*, he thought, feeling sorrowful that they were faced with such sickness during the holidays. He glanced at the time, excusing himself to help get ready for the dinner. "I'll see you all there, won't I?"

Ruth answered for them all, promising to "be there with bells on!"

Talia had curled up in bed with Titus, both of them winding down. "Looks like a nap might be in order between now and then." Dexter smiled warmly at the pair, and then stood to leave. He waded through the paper and ribbons, and promised to send housekeeping with some trash bags.

Dexter and Christina worked alongside countless other volunteers to create an ambience that camouflaged the sterility of the environment and the uncertainty of their plight. All of that was suspended in the presence of twinkling lights, poinsettias, holly, and even mistletoe. Families were seated together and served a traditional homemade feast. Dexter introduced Christina to the members of Titus' family that she hadn't met yet, and then elicited giggles from both Titus and Talia when he grabbed a sprig of mistletoe and held it over Christina's head. He waggled his eyebrows up and down theatrically and winked at Titus. Christina played along with the merriment and allowed herself to be kissed soundly.

Later that night, Dexter joined Christina to feed and rock babies and then she accompanied him to visit Titus and his family. They found only Ruth and Titus in the room. Titus was lying on his side, eyes fixed on the tree lights. He must be totally wiped out after such a hectic day. Ruth looked up from her knitting, a spreading smile causing her eyes to crinkle warmly. "Come in!"

Titus rolled over to see who his nana was talking to. His face lit up, but he made no move to sit up. "Hey, buddy," Dexter said to Titus, and then to Ruth, "Where's everyone else?"

"Jack and Lisa took Talia home. I think Jack will be back later." She cast a concerned eye toward Titus. "Ty needed a break from all the stimulation, so we thinned the crowd a little."

"It's been a big day," Christina said.

"Yeah, we just wanted to check in and say goodnight," Dexter added.

"We were hoping you'd come by," Ruth said. She looked at Dexter. "I felt such comfort when you prayed with me last night," she said, "would you mind?"

Christina looked up into Dexter's face, beaming. "Of course not!" the two of them said simultaneously.

The three adults, in unspoken agreement, gathered around Titus' bed. The child looked small and frail lying there. The four of them held hands, and Dexter led them in a prayer of thanksgiving, a prayer for healing. Three of the four of them ended with an amen. The fourth, Titus, retched violently, spilling the contents of his stomach onto the bed and floor.

Christina and Ruth jumped into action while Dexter stood dumbfounded for a beat. Ruth pressed the call button and was comforting Titus while Christina wet a washcloth and brought it over to him. When the nurse answered the call button, Ruth said, "We have a mess and need a little help."

"I thought his hand felt a little warm," Christina fretted.

Ruth pressed a hand to the child's forehead. She frowned. "You're right." Titus was silent, but didn't look good. Dexter realized that he had seen a change in him throughout the day, but had chalked it up to all the excitement. As a nurse aide shuffled in through the door, Ruth spoke again to Dexter and Christina. "We'll get him cleaned up and checked out. You guys go on and get some rest."

"You'll keep us posted, won't you?" Christina asked.

"Absolutely."

There was no mistaking the worry in Ruth's eyes, Dexter realized. He supposed even typical childhood ailments were something to be feared when the child was already fighting for his life. When they got into the hall, he asked Christina, "How serious do you think this is?"

She shrugged. "Could just be overexertion or rich Christmas food...or both." Nothing more was said until they were on the elevator. "If he's running a fever though..." Her voice trailed off, the rest of the sentence remaining unsaid.

They stopped by a couple of rooms that showed signs of activity. Youngsters begged them in, eager to show off Christmas gifts. Dexter and Christina happily obliged, staying to read stories or play with a new toy and give a tired parent or grandparent a chance to go for a cup of coffee or something. Dexter was grateful for the diversion from his thoughts, which kept going back to Titus. Once they were back in the room where they would sleep, Dexter checked his phone. There was nothing from Ruth, so he sent a text message asking how he was. The reply came within a minute or two.

Sorry. Lots of calls. His fever is pretty high. Have Jack here now. Just remember him in your prayers and maybe all will seem better in the morning.

Dexter showed his phone to Christina. "I guess we'd better get to praying," she said. And they did. They prayed an exhausting prayer, and when they couldn't

166

sleep an hour later they prayed again. Christina pulled out her Bible and they read from James. *Confess your faults one to another, and pray one for another, that ye may be healed. The effectual fervent prayer of a righteous man availeth much.* Dexter finally fell asleep, still praying.

He awoke to Christina brushing her teeth. It was barely daylight, but he knew she would be ready to see her babies in the nursery. He squinted at his phone. There was a message from Lisa that caused his heart to lurch.

Ty's fever spiked and he began seizing. He's unresponsive, but his temp is under control now. His labs are all over the place. Prayers appreciated.

Dexter thought back to the day before. How could this have happened so quickly?! He shared the unwelcome news with Christina. "What should we do?" he asked, adding, "I feel so helpless."

"Everyone does. I think that's the worst part."

They debated about how to proceed. In the end, they prayed for Ty's healing and asked God's comfort for the family. Christina went to see her babies, and Dexter headed to Ty's floor. He hesitated at the door, not wanting to intrude while the family was in crisis. He rapped softly and waited for a response. Jack pulled the door open and greeted him with a firm handshake and a clap on the back. "Hey, man, good to see you."

"How is he?"

"Well, we don't know for sure, but he's a fighter. The doc thinks the coma thing may be what his body needs to do to recuperate from everything."

"So…" Dexter was not satisfied with the answer. There had to be more.

"So, we wait," Lisa chimed in with a weak smile.

"How can I help?" Dexter wanted to know.

"Your presence is a big help. Your prayers... can you get others to pray for our son?" she said.

"I'll activate our prayer chain and get my family, Christina's family, our pastors to pray."

"That's awesome, man," Jack said gratefully. "Thanks!"

Dexter spent much of the morning on the phone with prayer warriors. When he had them in action, he checked in on Jack and Lisa. He encouraged them to go eat some lunch at lunchtime, promising to stay with Titus. Reluctantly, they went. Dexter used that time to talk to Titus and read to him. Christina showed up a time or two. And so the day passed. There was little change in Titus, and Dexter didn't know where the day had gone. He and Christina were supposed to leave the next day, but that was unthinkable. How could he leave with Ty lying there like that?

As the afternoon wore on, Dexter began to help pack away trees, lights, ornaments, stockings, and the like. When he got things boxed up, room by room, he set each of them in a corner of the room. In the nursery, Christina was doing the same thing. All of this stuff had been donated, and he had no idea if there was a plan in place for storing it. A quick text message confirmed what he might have suspected all along... his fiancé was on top of it.

We have a volunteer who can store it all in his warehouse. They're coming to pick up the first load at 5.

He looked at his phone. 4:37. He sent a reply.

Heading to Ty's room. LMK when they're here. I'll help.

Only Lisa sat next to Titus. She held his small hand, her head resting on the bed. Was she asleep? Praying? Dexter hesitated, but eventually entered the room quietly. At the sound of Dexter sitting down, Lisa lifted her head. She gave him a dazed half-smile.

"Any change?" he asked.

"No, not yet." she said. "His temperature is staying down though."

"That's encouraging. We're taking down some of the Christmas decorations. First load is being picked up in a few minutes. Do you want…?" The unfinished question dangled there sadly between them.

"I hate to," she said simply. There was nothing more for a moment, and then, "He enjoys the lights so much."

"Then let's keep them for when he wakes up."

Lisa studied Dexter for a moment, considering him. He must have looked a little puzzled under her scrutiny. "Thank you for saying 'when,'" she said finally.

He answered with only a smile. They sat there in silence until Dexter's phone buzzed. "I'm going to help load up some stuff. When I'm done, I'd be happy to hang with Ty while you get out for a bite to eat or whatever."

"That's nice," she said, "but I can't leave him."

"Then I can run and get you whatever sounds good," he offered.

She shook her head and started to argue, but then just said, "I'm not picky. Thank you."

Christina jumped right in and helped with loading the truck and then Dexter was able to persuade her to go out for dinner in the name of bringing sandwiches back for parents in a similar situation to Lisa's. Unfortunately, there were many. When they shared their intentions with the folks at Chik-fil-a, the establishment donated fifty sandwiches on top of the twenty they purchased. Dexter was amazed. He and Christina took great pleasure in distributing them at the hospital and were quick to give the restaurant credit.

They visited with Lisa and Ty for a bit, talking and praying. Titus was holding steady, but gave no indication of waking. They parted reluctantly and visited the nursery before turning in. Dexter couldn't bear the thought of leaving to return home while Ty's condition was so precarious, but they almost had to leave the next day as planned due to other obligations.

Dexter and Christina lay quietly in their separate beds after prayer, sleep eluding them. The sound of his phone buzzing at 1:30 a.m. struck terror in his heart. He scrambled to look at it, and then held it, squinting, incredulous. "He's awake!"

Christina sat upright as he rushed to show her his phone. A photo from Lisa displayed a crooked smile on a partially upright Titus -- the answer to prayer.

Someone wants to see you.'

"God, thank You. Thank You for hearing our pleas. Lord, I believe You for complete healing of this child. Nothing is impossible with You. I know You're going to make him well, and I praise You for it!" He muttered the prayer in a near delirious state.

Christina was already donning her shoes and pulling her hair into a ponytail. "Let's go!"

~~~~~~~~~

They spent the next three hours visiting with their little friend and his mother. Titus facetimed his dad, who was home with Talia. It had to be torture, Dexter mused, the way they had to divide up to take care of the sick and the well. Everyday life doesn't get suspended when there's an illness to be dealt with. School, work, monthly bills, haircuts, grocery shopping -- it all had to go on.

Finally, exhaustion took over, and Dexter stood to return to his room. He and Christina promised to spend more time with Titus before they left for home. After a few hours of sleep and a good breakfast, both Titus and Dexter were upright and playing a game when Christina joined them. Jack, Lisa, Talia, and Ruth were all present and overjoyed that their beloved Ty was awake and improving. They also wanted to see Dexter and Christina before their departure.

"You'll facetime me, right?" Ty asked Dexter.

"Of course!" he agreed readily, and then leaned in closer. Conspiratorially, he near whispered, "You work on getting better, so you can come to my wedding."

Titus grinned. "Are you going to kiss her again?"

"Yes, I am… every chance I get!"

The whole room heard and got a laugh out of that. Parting was difficult. There was so much uncertainty surrounding Titus' health. But with the promise of frequent messages and facetime sessions, he and Christina pulled themselves away.

Chapter Eighteen

"I think something's going on with them," Blair revealed after asking if Dexter had spoken with Spencer or Paula since his return from the mission trip. He hadn't. Not yet.

"What do you mean?"

"I went by on Christmas and things seemed...I don't know... a little tense. And then I called last night to see if they wanted to go to Sally's for pie, and they said 'no'.... Don't you think that's a little odd?"

Dexter rolled his eyes at his gossipy sister. "Yeah," he said dramatically, "if they don't want pie, then something *must* be going on!"

"Will you be serious?"

"Well, what did they say exactly? What makes you think there's something wrong?"

"Paula said she had eaten so much pie during the holidays that the thought of it made her a little queasy."

"Blair.... That sounds totally legit." He was puzzled.

"But when I asked if Spencer would want to go," Blair paused for effect (he assumed) and then whispered theatrically, "she told me to just text him and ask."

"So they must have not been in the same place," Dexter tried.

"I asked." Of course she did. "Paula said they were both at home, but he was downstairs and she was upstairs."

"That makes sense. No need for her to be the go-between when you could just ask him yourself."

"I guess," she admitted reluctantly. She looked at Dexter. "But Spencer declined too."

"Spencer said no to pie?"

"Mm hmm," Blair said, arching an eyebrow.

"I see what you mean then," Dexter said, only half-joking. "Something *does* seem a little off."

"Right?!"

Well, they'd find out soon enough. Paula and Christina had discussed New Year's Eve plans, and no doubt, they'd all be together. Christina was hosting this time since Paula had hosted Thanksgiving. Blair voiced plans to bring sausage balls, white chocolate cranberry cookies, and Rob. Apparently Dexter had not spooked him away. It's bad enough to bring a new boyfriend to a wedding, but to have a proposal there too? Dexter thought it might have been a little too much. He was either strong of heart or had already lost his heart. Time would tell which.

Meanwhile, Dexter and Christina were trying to catch up on responsibilities that had been postponed while they were away. That, and catch up on rest. Dexter was physically tired because, he realized upon reflection, neither he nor Christina had slept much. One could function on three or four hours of sleep a night for a few days, but would have to catch up eventually. And beyond the physical fatigue, he was emotionally drained. He had put so much into pulling off the perfect proposal, and *that* whole evening was emotionally charged. And then there was the mission trip. Nothing could have prepared him for the havoc that would wreak on his heart. Dexter had visited the hospital before, and had helped in so many ways -- he thought he was ready. But there's just something different about diving in and living among the patients and families for a few days.

He couldn't get little Titus off his mind. The boy had left an impression on him that tugged on his heartstrings. And he had so many other things hopping around in the back of his mind as well. He was a newly engaged man, and hadn't even had a chance to relish the fact that Christina was going to be his wife. They had so many decisions to make! They hadn't set a date or decided where to live or anything. Hopefully, things would slow down soon as they eased into the new year and they could get down to the business of planning their future.

~~~~~~~~~~

"How do you do that?" Dexter was marveling at the spread of snack foods that was accumulating on a festive table.

"Do what?" Christina asked, following his gaze but seeing nothing remarkable.

"*That*," he said gesturing at the table as if it should be obvious. "And that," he said, pointing to where the Christmas tree had stood two days ago. "And all this," he said, waving an arm to indicate all the streamers. She had returned from a heart-wrenching mission trip, taken down Christmas decorations, jumped back into work responsibilities, shopped for groceries, prepared food, and beaten the house into shape for a New Year's Eve party. "I hope the kids helped, 'cause I know I didn't have a hand in it." He hated to think of her working this hard on her own.

"I sent Lily to the store," she offered with a chuckle, "and Payton helped me take the tree down and put everything away."

"I would've helped."

"I know. You had your own catching up to do though."

He supposed that was true enough, but they were going to be a team. Dexter needed her to know that he was willing to help with whatever she needed done. He told her as much, to which she responded with a kiss and "ditto."

Christina only stood still for a moment. As she darted around the kitchen, Dexter shared that he had heard from Ruth.

Christina stopped what she was doing and faced Dexter, "How's Titus doing?"

"Good, I think. I mean, they take it day by day because -- as we saw on Christmas -- things can change fast. But so far, so good."

Christina nodded, understanding that such situations warranted cautious optimism. It was a relief that there had been good days since last week's scare. "Will he be up for facetiming to meet the family later?" They had talked about the possibility, hoping Titus would feel up to it and want to.

Dexter grinned. "Yeah, and not only that....but he also wants to ring in the new year with us!"

"Are you serious?" When Dexter nodded, Christina asked, "And what does Lisa say about him staying up until midnight?"

"I think we're going to facetime when everyone gets here, and then hopefully he'll rest. They'll wake him up to see in the new year." He thought for a moment, and then added, "I don't think she would say much anyway -- even if he doesn't rest in between."

Christina pulled in a deep breath and released it. "It must be difficult with a sick child… trying to parent the way you would if they weren't sick. I mean, you want to believe that the outcome will be good, but when you know your child has an illness that could take his life before he reaches adulthood… I don't know. Things like bedtime and manners and eating your vegetables seem trivial when he's fighting for his life. It would be easy to let a lot of things go."

He nodded his understanding. "They do a beautiful job at picking their battles without spoiling him. It can't be easy to balance it out."

"Well, Titus is pretty special. Some children take to spoiling and might even milk a situation like this. Titus isn't like that."

"He is a great kid, isn't he?"

"He is," Christina agreed.

Haley and Jared were the first to arrive, followed closely by Jordan and Brianna. Payton and Lily had been in and out the whole time. Paula carried some food down from next door.

"Where's Spence?" Dexter asked.

"He went to get some soft drinks," Paula replied.

"That reminds me," Christina interjected, looking at Dexter, "do you mind filling the ice stand? There's a bag of ice in the freezer."

"Sure."

Christina looked back to Paula. "Do you have more to carry from your house? I can help."

"A few things, if you're not too busy."

"You didn't cook a bunch, did you? Haley and Brianna brought food, and Blair is supposed to…"

Paula's laughter cut her off. "We just can't help ourselves, can we? Everything we celebrate involves food and lots of it!"

"Isn't that the truth?! Melissa will probably bring something too, and if Gail and Becca come, they probably won't be empty-handed."

"We won't go hungry, thats for sure!" Paula chuckled, opening the back door. "Not all of it's food though. I thought I'd bring a couple of games."

"Oh, yes," Christina replied. "That's a good idea."

The two women puttered around the kitchen for a few minutes, gathering the prepared food and the board games. Paula had the lion's share of it, with Christina carrying only the games. They were almost to the edge of the yard when Paula remembered something she had forgotten. "Oh shoot," she said, "I forgot the spicy mustard that Spencer likes with Blair's sausage balls."

"I'll go back for it," Christina offered. "I have a lighter load. Just tell me where to find it."

Paula conceded, telling her where it was located. Christina trekked back across the yard, and was able to locate a fresh jar of the specified mustard in the cabinet. She turned the light off and turned to leave, bumping right into Spencer. A million thoughts went through her mind, not the least of which was the fact that they were alone in the house together. That wasn't good.

"Spencer -- you scared the daylights out of me!"

"What a pleasant surprise," he said with an unreadable, but intense expression on his face.

"I know how it looks," Christina said, taking a stab at humor, "but I'm really not stealing your board games."

"What *are* you doing then?"

"I was helping Paula carry things down to my house, and came back to get this." She held up the mustard. "She said you like it. I've never tried it." She was rambling nervously, but couldn't seem to help it. This was Dexter's brother, but they couldn't be more different. Christina couldn't believe she had ended up alone with him.

He studied her for a moment, unmoving. Finally, he stepped aside. "You should definitely try it. It's great with those sausage ball things."

Christina breathed a sigh of relief. "I will," she said, and then, "Well, I should be getting back home."

"What's your hurry?"

"Well, it's kind of important for the hostess to be there." She chuckled apprehensively.

He took a step closer to her. "I think it's kind of important for you to be here with me."

"Spencer…"

"Don't you see how fate keeps throwing us together?" He was closing in on her. "Let me give you a better taste of Billings."

Panicked, she called out to no one, hoping to fake him out. "Dexter? Is that you?"

Spencer paused, but a slow, menacing smile spread across his face. "Baby brother's not here to save you from what's destined to happen, Christina."

He reached for her with apparent intent to kiss her. "No!" Christina screamed, slamming the games into his chest. Games pieces and pretend money flew everywhere.

She used the diversion to duck away from him and make a beeline for the door. She reached for the handle, but it was locked. Spencer's hand dug into her arm. "Leave me alone!" she shouted, jerking away from his grasp. Finally, Christina pulled the door open and found herself face to face with Paula.

Everyone froze momentarily. Christina was certain Paula had seen most of what had just happened, but she gave no outward indication. Her voice was frighteningly calm when she spoke. "Oh good, you found it." Paula picked up the mustard from where Christina had set it down on the counter top. Her gaze moved over the scattered game pieces. She turned to leave, calling back over her shoulder, "Spence, bring the games when you come."

Christina was flabbergasted to the point of immobilization. But she certainly didn't want to be left alone with Spencer, so she called her legs to action and hurried to catch up with Paula. Her neighbor and friend walked with long, purposeful strides, covering the distance between their two homes too quickly to allow discussion of the preceding incident. "Paula..." Christina began.

Paula stopped abruptly, and took a deep breath in and out before speaking. She met Christina's troubled gaze with tear-shiny eyes. "It's okay," she said. "I'm okay."

"Paula..." Christina tried again, but found no other words.

"I know."

Christina took her friend in her arms. "I'm so sorry."

Paula let herself be held briefly, returning the embrace. "I'm going to head straight to your bathroom. I need to compose myself. Can we just pretend nothing happened? Just for tonight?"

"Of course," Christina said, "Whatever you need."

Paula pulled back, wiped her eyes, and said, "We'll talk soon, I promise."

"I'm here when you're ready."

Once inside, Christina ushered Paula to the bathroom off her own bedroom in the interest of privacy. Though she was still shaken herself, she took a deep breath and jumped into hostess mode. Haley was in the kitchen. At first sight of her mother, concern clouded her face. "Are you okay?"

"Yeah, why?"

"I don't know. You just look...well, out of sorts."

Christina brushed it off, assured her daughter she was fine, and thanked God Dexter wasn't around. She would have never been able to fool him. She didn't plan to keep it from him, but it was a conversation for later. She threw herself into the tasks at hand, and bolstered by Paula's practiced simulation of normalcy, carried on as if nothing had happened. Even when Spencer came in with games and soft drinks a little while later, Christina just cheerfully announced that they could facetime Titus now that the gang was all here. She did, however, stick like glue to Dexter and avoid making eye contact with Spencer.

~~~~~~~~~~

"Hey, buddy!" Dexter said when Ty's face filled the iPad screen. He looked good, Dexter thought -- a far cry from the way he looked a week ago.

"Hi," Titus said, and then immediately, "I miss you. When are you coming back?"

Dexter laughed a little, his heart warmed by the boy's words. "I'll talk to Christina. We'll work out a day trip sometime in the next couple of weeks, okay?" When Titus agreed, Dexter went on. "Tonight though, you get to meet the rest of our motley crew!" One by one, Dexter introduced every family member and friend that was present, passing the ipad around and giving everyone a chance to say hello. They ended the session after about thirty minutes with a promise of reconnecting just shy of midnight.

The evening progressed smoothly, with a few friends dropping by for a while but not staying to see the new year in. At one point Dexter asked Haley if her mother seemed okay. "I thought she seemed a little preoccupied too, but she said she was fine when I asked," Haley revealed.

"Probably just trying to get everything ready and make sure the guests have a good time," Dexter suggested. Haley agreed. They both looked over in the direction of a heated game of Taboo, where Christina and Paula seemed to be having a blast. Spencer had ducked out early, saying he wasn't feeling well. Dexter couldn't say he was disappointed about that. He loved his brother, but still wasn't crazy about him being around Christina. Blair and Rob played Uno with Jordan and Brianna. All around the room and spilling into the downstairs den, friends and family enjoyed snacks, good company, and recreation. The time passed easily, and Dexter was surprised when someone commented that they had only ten minutes to say goodbye to the year.

Dexter sent a quick text message to Lisa asking if Titus was ready. Five minutes later, his iPad lit up with an incoming facetime call. When he answered, a sleepy little boy filled the screen. Soon they were all counting down to the big moment and welcoming in the new year. Dexter passed the iPad to Paula and took Christina in his arms, kissing her softly. This was only a dream last year, and he thanked God that this year it was a dream come true.

Chapter Nineteen

On January 2nd, Dexter received a surprising message from his sister-in-law. Actually, it was a group message including him, Christina, and Blair.

I'd like to talk to you guys. Could we meet at Christina's this evening?

How odd! One by one, everyone replied in the affirmative and a time was agreed upon. Noting that his brother was not included in the group message, Dexter couldn't help but wonder if Spencer had done something. What if Paula was gathering them to say that they were splitting up? He recalled Blair saying that she thought something was going on with them. As if by cue, his sister sent a private message.

Do you know what this is about?

He told her that he did not. Christina was conspicuously quiet about it, even when he saw her later in the day. And so Dexter waited until the appointed time. They would all find out together. He carried on about his day, stayed busy, and tried not to wonder about it too much. After work, he headed over to Christina's. He found that Paula was already there, almost as if she wanted to save Christina from having to field questions in her absence. They had no more than greeted each other until Blair's car turned into the driveway.

Christina had a pot of coffee brewing, and everyone gravitated toward the kitchen. They made small talk until everyone had a cup of coffee sitting on the table in front of them. Though Dexter and Blair tried not to, they both ended up looking expectantly at Paula when Christina finally joined them at the kitchen table. Dexter watched as Christina gave Paula's hand a reassuring squeeze. This was going to be major, he realized. What had his brother done now?

Paula took a deep breath and began, "This is going to affect all of us, and I don't want to have to repeat it." She looked around the table at each of them. "You know I love Spencer, and I don't think it's any secret that I've had to look the other way through the years."

Blair looked at Dexter and then at Paula. "You knew?" Paula squeezed her eyes shut and nodded her head. Yes, she had known. Maybe not everything, but after all the years of wondering if she knew how he was with women, now they finally knew that she did. A quiver full of emotions pierced Dexter, one after the other, without giving him time to process. Sadness, disappointment, anger, pity, uncertainty, relief. Such little had been said so far, but so much had been revealed. But why now?

"Has something happened, Paula? What's going on?" Dexter asked gently.

"We had only been married three months the first time I saw Spencer flirting with a girl we had gone to school with. He told me it wasn't how it looked, that I was letting my insecurity show. We argued, but in the end he convinced me that I was more at fault than he was."

"He's a smooth-talker, that's for sure," Blair said.

"The first time I found proof that there had been more than flirting, I was devastated. This time, he didn't try to talk his way out of it. He fell to his knees and swore he only loved me. He said he didn't know why he had done it and begged me not to leave him. The next time, he said he couldn't explain it, that he didn't think he was like other men. He said he loved me more than anything and that it had nothing to do with that. He made it sound like some kind of compulsion that was practically beyond his control. I know no one could understand -- sometimes I don't understand it myself -- but he was so..." She paused, searched for words to convey what she saw in him. "...distraught and sincere. I thought I would die from the betrayal, but he was so attentive and convincing."

Paula looked up. Her eyes were dry, tears over these matters long since shed and wiped. Dexter and Blair looked at her with concern, but said nothing. Christina sipped her coffee and then patted Paula's hand. Paula went on. "I don't expect anyone to understand. But I love Spencer, and as crazy as it sounds, I know he loves me. Once the decision was made to stay together after the second time, I knew that I was probably signing up for a lifetime of these incidents. I also knew that I was in it alone." When they each started to protest, Paula held up her hand. "Not even you guys would understand me staying by his side under these circumstances. I couldn't have stood the pity." She pulled in a breath and let it out as a sigh. "So I kept it to myself. I did a lot of looking the other way, and Spencer and I have done a lot of talking. But things kept happening. It was like an impulse that he couldn't suppress."

When she paused again, Blair spoke. "Paula, I can't believe you've been dealing with this on your own for all these years!"

"I spoke to a pastor once or twice, but could never get Spencer to go. We were both so ashamed. I wish I had set my foot down a long time ago, but I guess it all had to unravel the way it has."

"Counseling might have helped," Dexter offered.

"Yes, I think it would have," Paula replied. "And I'm pinning a lot of hopes on it now." She pulled a pamphlet from a pocket and opened it carefully. "Apparently there's such a thing as 'sex addiction.' It says here that it is 'characterized by compulsive searching for multiple partners or fixation on unattainable partners.'" She glanced up at Christina sheepishly.

Dexter stood up suddenly. "Has something else happened?" he demanded, looking first at Christina then at Paula. His gaze landed back on Christina and his voice gentled, "Did he hurt you?"

"Woah!" Blair chimed in. "He tried something with Christina?!"

Christina looked tremendously uncomfortable. "Um... There have been a few incidents, but no one got hurt...well, not physically at least." She looked directly at Dexter. "Paula witnessed the exchange the other night. Please know that I wasn't trying to keep secrets from you..."

Paula jumped in to explain, "I just needed some time to process, and I asked Christina to wait before she said anything."

"And I figured that if Paula could pretend everything was okay for a little while, then I could too," Christina said.

He sat back down, still stewing, trying to understand. "What else does it say? I've heard there was such a thing, but never thought it could apply to Spence."

Paula held up the pamphlet again. "It says that sex addiction involves 'engaging in persistent and escalating patterns of sexual behavior acted out despite increasing negative consequences to self and others.'" She laid the pamphlet down and looked up at Dexter. "Think about how this particular part of Spencer doesn't match up with the rest. He is a loving and generous man -- with a tremendous flaw. But I think there's hope for addressing the flaw and getting things under control. I've done some research, and there are lots of treatment options."

"Will he go?" Blair asked.

"He will if he wants to stay married to me," Paula declared, surprising everyone at the table, though not unpleasantly. "I should have given the ultimatum years ago. I let pride get in the way, and now neither of us has any of that left. Everyone in town knows how he is. I can hardly even show my face at Sally's anymore -- he flirts shamelessly and everyone knows it. But they don't know the rest of the story. That's between Spence and me...and God."

Christina agreed, "That's exactly right. People will form opinions based on what they think they know. In this case, they know very little. Pay no attention to them. You do what you feel in your heart to be right, what God is directing you to do."

Dexter softened at Christina's words. "She's right," he said. "No one else has the whole story and no one else has to live with the outcome. Staying focused on your marriage and God's will for it is your best bet."

Blair only nodded, adding nothing more to what the others had said. Paula thanked them for being supportive and shared that there was a residential treatment program with Christian counseling and good results. "If all goes well, we can follow up with outpatient counseling and maybe a couples retreat in the spring. I'm more hopeful than I've been in a long time."

"Where is he now?" Dexter asked.

"He's at home. He's been making arrangements to be off work for the inpatient stay."

"Does he know you're telling us about it all?"

"Yeah, I told him that it was time. He's going to want to talk to you, Dex. I thought maybe you could drive him to the facility tomorrow. It's about an hour and a half from here, and it would be a good chance to talk. Would you do that?"

"Of course," Dexter agreed without hesitation.

"Listen, I know that when we part that you all will look up more information about this. You'll read a lot of disgusting things. I don't want to make you uncomfortable, but I want you guys to know that to my knowledge there hasn't been a lot of pornography or deviant stuff. And because it's only natural to wonder, I should tell you that Spence and I have enjoyed a healthy and satisfying intimate relationship throughout our marriage. From what I've read, that doesn't necessarily matter."

There were hugs around the room before they parted. When Dexter hugged Blair, he admonished quietly, "Don't you go telling any of this. Paula kept this to herself for a long time and I don't want any of us to make her regret sharing with us."

"I won't!" Blair replied indignantly, as if the request weren't warranted.

Once Blair and Paula left, Dexter and Christina sat down on her couch. There she began to fill him in on the details of what had happened on New Year's Eve and even the incident at Sally's that night some time back. He was very quiet, not quite knowing which of his swirling emotions to embrace. It angered him to think of his brother putting Christina into these situations where she felt intimidated and afraid. It was disappointing and embarrassing. Yet he loved Spencer and believed he had many good qualities.

"Do you believe that Spencer planned to put you in those situations?" Dexter asked.

"You mean was it premeditated?" she asked with a smirk.

Dexter chuckled, "Yeah, I guess."

Christina thought for a moment before answering. "No, I don't think so," she said eventually. "I think he just mishandled it once we were alone together."

Dexter blew out a breath of air. It was a lot to process, but he was certainly glad to be able to speak openly with Paula about it. For years, he had wondered how much she knew of Spencer's antics. Could it really be that all those antics were attributable to an actual disorder? He never wanted to believe his brother was a scoundrel, though his behavior said otherwise at times. Dexter was more than a little relieved to have it all on the table and to have the hope of treatment through counseling.

"I'm sorry that he has done you that way -- especially the last couple of incidents. I never meant for him to even have a chance."

"I always just hated it so much for Paula's sake," Christina answered. "I was afraid she would misread the situation and think I was leading him on or something."

He nodded, understanding. "Maybe it's all behind us now."

"I'm optimistic," she said brightly.

~~~~~~~~~~

The new year certainly brought change. Haley began the year settling into her new role as a wife. Spencer and Paula began to seek healing and unity in their marriage. The next transition presented itself a couple of weeks into January when Jordan and Brianna got snowed in at Christina's. Dexter stayed over too, though to be honest, he could have made it back to his place. Christina wanted him to err on the side of caution though, and he obliged.

The snow started to fall, but little accumulation was predicted. Christina put on a pot of chili and invited the kids over. Jared and Haley were the first to arrive and the first to leave when it was obvious the snow was going to stick. Dexter was amused, realizing that they were typical newlyweds and didn't relish the idea of spending the night in close proximity of others. Payton and Lily had been there all afternoon, but Lily left with Haley and Jared. They would drop her off on their way home. Jordan and Brianna didn't pay too much attention to the weather, knowing they could stay over if they needed to. A blanket of sparkling white covered the ground while they ate and then played Scrabble.

Between games, Dexter suggested checking in with Titus. With everyone in agreement, he shot a text message to Lisa to ask if it was a good time. Her response was an incoming facetime call, which Dexter gladly took.

"Hey there, Ty! How's it going?"

"Good. Check this out!" Titus held up a Luke Skywalker action figure.

"That's awesome!" Dexter said.

Christina joined Dexter, peering over his shoulder. "Hey, Titus! I thought you had Luke Skywalker already."

"I did, Ms. Christina, but look how much better this one looks." The boy held up both the old one and the new one for the sake of comparison.

Dexter and Christina both inspected the figures, one brand new and the other having seen hours and hours of play. And then Dexter noticed something else. The walls behind him were blue, not like the hospital room he had been in before.

"Have you moved to a different room?" he asked.

Titus looked confused. "No, this is my same old room."

"But the walls are blue."

"The walls have always been blue. It's my favorite color."

It was Christina for whom it all clicked into place. "Titus, are you home now?!"

"Oh yeah, I am! I forgot that you didn't know."

"That's wonderful!" Dexter said. "Are you feeling good? I bet you're glad to be back in your own bed."

"I'm feeling fine. Let me show you around."

By this time, the rest of the family had gathered around, joining the tour of Ty's bedroom. The walls were a cheery blue, topped with a Star Wars border. The room was filled with little boy things -- ball gear, Star Wars memorabilia, posters, etc. They all chatted about wonderfully mundane things, Titus' health not appearing to be an issue of concern at this point. When the call ended a few minutes later, Dexter and Christina marveled at how good Titus looked and how thrilled they were that he was home. Dexter vowed to get the scoop from Ruth or Lisa the next day.

Meanwhile, Brianna emerged from the bathroom looking a little gray. She waved off Christina's concerns, saying that she was fine, just tired. Christina provided a gown for her daughter-in-law to sleep in and ushered her to bed in Haley's old room. Jordan stayed up a while longer. Scrabble and hot cocoa filled the next hour. Dexter sent messages to Blair and Paula ascertaining that they were safely in out of the weather. They were. With Christina's permission, he told Paula she should come on over and join them. Spencer was still away for inpatient treatment. She declined though, already in pajamas.

After Jordan and Payton shuffled off to bed, Dexter opened the front door and looked out at the snow. The cold air was invigorating, and the whole world seemed to have hushed under the blanket of white. Christina stood next to him, pulling his arm around her for warmth. "Isn't it beautiful?" she breathed.

"It is. There's nothing like it."

"The kids were always so eager to get out and play in it, but I love it when it's like this -- freshly fallen and uninterrupted. I hated to see it marred."

"I know what you mean," he said.

They stood in silence until the cold air forced them in. Christina yawned. "I hate for the night to end, but I'm wearing down," she admitted.

"It's been a great evening."

"Would you rather sleep downstairs or here on the couch?"

"The couch is fine," he said. When Christina brought a pillow and a quilt, he took them and pulled her in for a kiss. "I'm getting pretty anxious for the time when we can head to the same bed."

Christina blushed slightly, but agreed. "We've got plans to make, don't we?"

"We sure do!"

"Let's get started on that tomorrow, shall we? I'm pretty eager myself," she said, raising a teasing eyebrow.

Dexter bedded down on the couch a few minutes later, taking time to thank God for the obvious improvement in his little friend's health. He thought about Christina lying in her bed just a few feet away. Walls separated them now, but soon they wouldn't have to. They had an entire future to look forward to together, and he couldn't wait to get started.

Chapter Twenty

Dexter awoke to the aroma of coffee and questionable sounds from the bathroom. He sat up, rubbing sleep from his eyes, and listened. He was pretty sure someone was sick behind the closed door. Wandering into the kitchen, he greeted Christina and asked if she knew who was in the bathroom.

"I'm not sure, but you can use one of the others."

"No, I can wait. It's just that it sounds like someone is sick."

Christina checked the bedrooms and determined that Brianna was the one missing. She rapped on the closed door. "Brianna?" There was a mumble from the other side. "Are you okay?"

Brianna opened the door a little and said, "Yeah, I'm fine." But she didn't look fine.

"You're sick," Christina observed. "Let me get you a wet washcloth."

Brianna stepped aside and let Christina into the bathroom. The older woman quickly retrieved a washcloth and wet it in cold water. Brianna took it from her and dabbed her face. "Thanks," she said weakly.

"I knew you didn't seem right last night. Is there anything I can do?"

"No, I'm fine. Really."

The pair of women emerged from the bathroom, but as soon as Brianna got a whiff of the coffee she was right back in front of the commode. Dexter and Christina looked at one another. "It's just the smell of the coffee," Brianna called back over her shoulder. "I'll be fine in a minute."

"That's the way it is when you're sick," Dexter said.

"Or when you're pregnant," supplied Christina.

Surprise registered on Dexter's face. "Do you think…?"

Christina smiled. "We'll soon find out!"

Brianna opened the door once again, standing there a few seconds to test the waters. "Why don't you lie back down?" Christina said. "I'll bring you some toast or something in a little while."

The younger woman nodded, padding off to the bedroom. Dexter jumped at the chance to duck into the bathroom while Christina poured him a cup of coffee. He sat down in the kitchen, sipping coffee and watching as she whipped up a batch of muffins.

"Have you thought about where you'd like to live?" Dexter asked while she stirred the batter.

Christina stopped and looked at him. "I *have* been thinking about that. I love my home, but I feel like it might be nice for us to start out in a home of our own. What do you think?"

"I'm not attached to my house. Lots of bad memories there. I like the idea of a fresh start, but I hadn't made any assumptions about you leaving your home. I'm open to anything."

"It would be a lot easier to leave here if it stayed in the family. I raised my kids here, planted the trees in the yard, and so on. I wondered if Jordan and Brianna might have any interest in buying it. Even if my hunch isn't right, they will probably need a bigger place eventually."

"And Haley and Jared can buy my place when she finishes her internship!" He was half-joking, but Christina's eyes lit up as if it were a real possibility.

"If it all works out, maybe we could build a home," Christina said.

"That sounds good, but will take time. Honestly, I want you to be my wife as soon as you're willing."

"Let's pray about it before we decide. We could brainstorm with the kids just to gauge their reaction. I don't want any delays either, but love the idea of making decisions about every little feature of our new home and life together."

"Between Spencer and me, we could do a lot of the work ourselves," Dexter said thoughtfully.

Payton stumbled through about that time. They all exchanged *good mornings*, though Payton had little more to contribute. He poured himself a glass of milk and started toward the living room. He turned back around, addressing his mother, "Did you know Jordan and Brianna are looking for a house?"

Christina paused from her task of pulling muffins from the oven, looking at him. "You're kidding…."

"No, Jordan said something about it last night. I don't know why they'd want to move. I think that apartment is a pretty sweet deal."

Christina glanced up at Dexter, who was sitting slack-jawed. She set the muffins down and turned back to Payton. "Well, you know… they wouldn't want to rent forever. And maybe they're thinking that a bigger place would be better."

"I guess. I'd love to have that apartment though," he said, his voice trailing off as he left the room.

Dexter was still reeling from the coincidence when Christina sat the basket of muffins on the table. Could it be that God was already setting things into motion? At the sound of someone else getting up, Christina put on some peppermint tea for Brianna and popped some bread in the toaster. Jordan ambled into the kitchen, heading directly for the coffeepot.

After a cursory greeting, Christina inquired as to whether Brianna was awake.

"She's awake, but she's not vertical," Jordan revealed.

"Still feeling rough?" Dexter asked.

"Yeah, pretty rough."

Christina plated the dry toast and stirred a little honey into the tea. As she walked out of the kitchen, Jordan asked what she was doing, she nonchalantly called back over her shoulder, "I'm taking your wife some peppermint tea and toast. It used to do wonders for *my* morning sickness."

Jordan just covered his face with his hand and shook his head. He neither confirmed nor denied his mother's speculation until she returned with Brianna fifteen minutes or so later. Dexter resisted the urge to needle him about it, instead scooting the muffin basket over to where the younger man had sat down. Both of them ate and talked about trivial things, primarily the snow. It brightened the room and gave the day a serene feel.

Dexter heard the women before he saw them, but couldn't tell what they were chatting about. When they entered the room, he was glad to see that Brianna's color looked better. She took a seat next to Jordan and whispered to him, "I had to tell her. She pretty much already knew, and I couldn't just straight out lie to her." Jordan smiled a broad smile and nodded knowingly. He would have done the same thing.

Jordan looked up at his mother with a grin. "We were dying to tell you anyway," he said.

Brianna added, for the benefit of everyone else, "Like I told Christina, we were trying to keep quiet about it until we hit the twelve week mark -- you know, just in case."

Christina was around the table and hugging Jordan before anyone knew what was what. "Seems like you should still be a baby yourself, and now you're going to have one of your own!" She pulled back and beamed at him. "You two are going to be wonderful parents!"

"Congratulations," Dexter said sincerely, clapping Jordan on the shoulder. He then turned to Payton, who had followed the chaos back into the kitchen. "What do you think about that? You're going to be an uncle!"

"Pretty cool," he replied, a smile spreading across his face.

Christina poured herself some fresh coffee and sat down. "How far along are you exactly?"

"Nine weeks and two days," Brianna said. Wow, Dexter thought, when Christina asked for *exactly* she got *exactly*!

Jordan pulled up a picture on his phone and turned it to show everyone. "This is what the baby looks like now." Dexter viewed the image that resembled a cross between an alien and some sort of legume, and was astonished to hear Brianna and Christina talking about how amazing it was. Not to seem impolite, he just smiled and withheld his thought that it had a long way to go!

"You'd better call your sister," Christina said. "She'll already be upset at being the last one to know."

"Well, if she would have stayed, she would have found out with everyone else. She shouldn't have been in such a hurry to get home!" Jordan grumbled, though he was dialing the phone at the same time.

Haley was ecstatic! After Jordan talked to her a few minutes, he passed the phone to his wife. While Brianna talked to Haley, Christina nudged Dexter. "It might be a good time to see how everyone feels about moving," she whispered.

He nodded in agreement. "Do you know if Jared was with her?" Dexter asked Jordan.

"Oh yeah, he was there. She told him everything I said," Jordan laughed.

Christina got Brianna's attention and told her not to hang up, that she wanted to talk to Haley. A minute later both phones were on speaker, and a family conference commenced.

"Dexter and I have started to talk about plans for our future...you know, where to live and all. We'd like to have input from all of you." After a chorus of sures and okays, she continued. "I don't want you all to feel like I'm turning my back on my past just because I'm embracing my future, but I don't think it's fair to ask Dexter to move in here where I lived with your father. I feel like we need to start fresh, both of us on neutral ground."

"That's understandable," came Haley's voice over the phone.

"Yeah, that's up to you guys," said Jordan.

Christina smiled. "Thank you, but doesn't it just break your heart to think of this house not being in the family? You all grew up here." There was murmur of agreement.

Dexter jumped in at that point. "If we buy or build a new home, we would have both this one and my house to sell. I know there's no sentimental attachment to my house, but it would be a terrific starter home for a new couple."

"And leaving here would be a lot easier to do if the house stayed in the family. You know -- we were just brainstorming, but we thought we'd see if there'd be any interest. Jordan, you and Brianna will need a bigger house now that your family is growing. Think about whether buying this house is something you'd want to consider."

Dexter spoke next. "Haley, you'll be finished with your internship in May. You guys won't want to stay in that little apartment once you begin your career. Think about whether you'd be interested in buying my house. I could even rent it to you for a while if a mortgage freaks you out this soon."

"And I could take your apartment," said Payton.

Christina turned to him. "Honey, I don't want you to feel displaced. You have a home with me wherever I am." Dexter nodded his agreement.

"Nah, I've been thinking about getting my own place anyway. It's time -- or it will be by the time you guys get married anyway."

"When *are* you all getting married?" Haley asked over the phone.

Dexter said, "Well, we don't know yet. We've just started talking about where to live. I guess setting a date might hinge on what we decide with that."

"Sometime this year though," Christina said, meeting Dexter's eyes with a smile.

"It's a lot to think about," Brianna said.

"And please don't feel any pressure if you don't feel like it's the right move. It's just one scenario to consider," Christina said.

In that manner, it was all left on the table for everyone to chew on. Dexter felt confident that God would work it out. He would be willing to sell his house and simply move in there, but the idea of a fresh start appealed to him a lot more. Yet he could understand Christina's reluctance to leave. Placing it in God's hand was all that he could do.

~~~~~~~~~~

On the cold winter days when work was slow, Dexter worked toward getting his house ready to go on the market. Small repairs and paint touch-ups would be appreciated by Haley and Jared even if it never officially made it onto the market. He worked on cleaning and organizing as well, thinking about what he would take with him and what he'd give up.

It was mid-February, and he still didn't have a definitive answer about how it was all going to go down. Jordan and Brianna seemed to be leaning toward buying Christina's house, which was a big relief. If they could get the ball rolling in the next month or so, Dexter could call in some favors and have a home ready for them to move into mid-summer. Then Jordan and Brianna might get moved in before the baby came. Lots of ifs, lots of mights. But he could pave the way by getting his house ready and talking about house plans with Christina.

He and Christina agreed to purchase a new bedroom suite and bedding. They didn't actually say it, but neither of them wanted to share a bed that had been shared with someone else. It was best to just spring for something new. As far as other furniture, they had talked about particular pieces to keep from each of their homes so that their new home would be a blend. His living room furniture was in better shape since there had been no children wearing it out. Christina had a new washer and dryer that she would bring with her. And so on. In that way, Dexter felt they were making progress.

He purchased some large totes, thinking that a lot of shelved items that were rarely used but needed to be kept could be packed in them. He began with closets, marveling at how much he had accumulated. Much of it was stuff Sarah had purchased, but had left behind in her hasty retreat. Dexter found photo frames and bedding. He came across photo albums that hadn't been touched in ages.

Dexter sat down in front of the hall closet and opened the first one he came to. On the first page was a photo of him and Sarah when they were dating. She looked so young and happy. *Was there really a time when she was happy with me?* Apparently so. As he turned the pages, he could see the contentment in both their faces, their courtship and early marriage documented with photos and ticket stubs from concerts and movies. He couldn't help but wonder what had happened to them. He felt that old fear creep back up into his heart. What made him think he could hold onto Christina's heart when he hadn't been able to hold onto Sarah's?

He picked up another photo album, this one containing mostly family snapshots and holiday events. Dexter scrutinized everyone's faces, especially Sarah's. Spencer's. His own. There were fewer of them together as a couple, and the ones he found told a different story than the first album. If the first had been titled *Discovery*, this one would surely have been titled *Complacency*. The final one he opened might have been *Disenchantment*. It was only half filled, its contents reminding Dexter that Sarah had fallen out of love with him. He supposed he had fallen out of love with her too. He studied the scowl on her face in one photograph. And what kind of expression did he wear? Perhaps a look of detachment. Dexter sighed and closed the album. He would have stuck it out, but in all honesty, he was now completely grateful to have been released from his vows.

Dexter refused to get bogged down in bad memories. What he needed was his touchstone. Christina's voice would make him feel better. He pulled out his phone and plopped onto the couch.

"I was just thinking about you," Christina said. He could *hear* her smiling. Immediately, his world felt right again, and all his doubts dissipated. This marriage would be different because Christina was different. And his feelings for her were different from anything he remembered experiencing before.

"Good thoughts?" he asked coyly.

"The best. I was thinking about how much I'm looking forward to being your wife."

"Sometimes I think I can't stand it, that I wish we could elope and that I'd live with you here or there or anywhere."

Christina's laughter had a nearly musical cadence. "You went all Dr. Seuss there!" she teased.

"I needed to hear your voice so badly. I've been trying to go through things here, and it's bringing me down."

"I know what you mean. Payton and I were looking through some stuff the other night. It's bittersweet."

"What do you even do with things like photo albums full of a couple that no longer exists? With no children, who would even want them? And yet, it is a part of my life and I hate to just burn them."

"Maybe Sarah would want them," Christina offered.

"I doubt it, but I do feel like I need to check with her before getting rid of some other things. I'll ask about the albums too."

Changing the subject, Christina brightened. "I have some good news."

"Let's have it," he said eagerly.

"Jordan and Brianna got approved for a home loan today and definitely want the house!"

"Christina, oh my gosh! That's terrific!"

"I know, right?! And I have something else to run past you…"

"O-kaay, go on."

"I wondered if you'd ever consider a fixer upper -- you know, as opposed to building. Melissa knows of someone whose mother just died and left behind a home that needs updating, This person isn't married and is perfectly content where she lives. She sees it as a headache, but it could be something wonderful."

Dexter immediately envisioned a 1950s ranch style house that would be difficult to build onto. Probably one bathroom and poor insulation. But you never know until you look. "I'll consider anything you want to consider. This is a joint venture."

"Great! I'll see if we can go have a look this weekend. Melissa sent a picture of it. I'll send it when we hang up. I think the lot it sits on is about two acres."

They chatted a little more about where it was located, and Dexter was intrigued. As they prepared to end the call, he reminded Christina to send the photo. He was taken aback when it came through. It was a generous two-story farmhouse with a wrap-around porch. It might need some work, but it was absolutely charming. Dexter sent a reply text.

Looks like it has potential!

Christina texted back **It's pretty old, but Melissa said they renovated in the 70s and has good plumbing.**

That was good, he thought. Hopefully the pipes were PVC. **I don't suppose it has CH&A?** he tapped out.

They had it installed for her in 2000.

It sounded more promising all the time, and he told her as much.

Melissa and the woman who owned the home, Annie, were waiting when Dexter and Christina pulled into the blacktopped driveway. The beautiful old home had a charm that couldn't be denied. The weatherboard siding was in desperate need of sprucing up, but that was only cosmetic. Dexter grabbed his clipboard and pencil as he got out of the truck so he could make notes about the work that would need to be done if they bought it. He walked around and opened the door for Christina, who was positively enchanted. "Would you just look at that porch?!" she exclaimed. Dexter was writing down *siding*, but glanced up to agree that the porch was a great feature.

It wrapped around three sides of the house and had a white railing. It begged for some furniture and a porch swing or two. He looked down at his clipboard and then scribbled *Needs* over the word *siding*. He headed a second column with a plus sign and beneath it wrote *porch, location, CH&A, blacktop.*

They greeted Melissa, who introduced them to Annie, a thin woman with salt-and-pepper hair. "Come on in," Annie said, stepping up onto the porch. She opened the screen door, which Dexter noted could stand to be updated. It was the old kind with a saggy screen. A modern door with a full panel of glass would perk the front up. He added it to the "needs" column, but put a question mark after it. It could wait, after all.

They stepped into the front room, which had beautiful hardwood floors and a blessed lack of wallpaper on the walls. He wrote *hardwood* in the plus column. And so it went from room to room. Linoleum covered the kitchen floor, and two of the bedrooms sported a ridiculous shag carpet. Annie assured them that hardwood was underneath it all.

"How many bathrooms are there?" Dexter asked.

"We just added one for Mother about five years ago. I'll show you," Annie said, leading them down the hallway. "We combined to bedrooms at the end of the hall to make a suite of sorts, adding a bathroom to make it easier for her."

"You said 'we.' Is there another sibling who may be interested in keeping the house?" Christina asked.

"No, I lost my only brother to cancer last year. There's no one but me, and I don't need all this. I'd love to see someone get it who could give it the love and attention it deserves."

"I'm sorry for your loss," Christina offered.

Annie nodded her thanks as she opened the door to her mother's suite. There was a gorgeous bed and armoire with a sitting area off to the side and a TV on the wall. The bathroom was small, but large enough for a generous tub with whirlpool jets in it. The walls were a mauve color. They all commented on how lovely it was.

"So, two bathrooms?" Dexter asked.

"Yes, but there's a space upstairs that could be converted."

Dexter and Christina asked more questions as they proceeded on their tour... how old is the roof? Is the foundation solid? Any problems with termites? And so on. Dexter continued to note things on his clipboard. Just when he thought they were finished, Annie opened a door and announced, "And this is the basement."

"There's a basement too?" Christina asked.

"Yes, but it's very basement-y," Annie warned. "Mother wasn't able to go up and down the steps these past few years, and I'm afraid we've let it go." They descended on bare steps lit by bare light bulbs. "It has never leaked or anything though, so maybe it would have potential with a good dehumidifier and some elbow grease."

Dexter and Christina grinned at one another. He liked this woman. The basement was unimpressive, but not alarming. Annie was right about the potential. Melissa, who had remained a silent observer much of the time, waited at the top of the stairs. They joined her and went out the back door to view an array of shade trees and a quaint little garden spot. He could tell that Christina was enchanted, and to be honest, he was too. While Christina listened attentively to Annie's explanation of where peonies and mums would grow in their due season, Dexter looked down at his clipboard. The plusses definitely outweighed the work that needed to be done. And the location could really grow on him. Christina would enjoy the gardening, and it would be fun to do the renovations together. Something about it was feeling right. He just hoped the price was.

Chapter Twenty-one

Dexter and Christina chatted excitedly all the way back to his house. There were so many possibilities, so many things they could do to the house to improve it. But when it came down to it, there was very little that *had* to be done before they moved in. That would be a relief... *if* they decided to take it. "It almost seems too good to be true," Christina commented breathily as they got out of the truck.

"You know what they say about that..." Dexter said.

"That *that's* when God has intervened on your behalf?" She grinned up at him, challenging him to disagree.

"Well, that's not what I was going to say...but that could be it."

Inside, Dexter grabbed bottles of water from the fridge and they got down to figuring the renovation expenses. Both of them had been surprised when Annie had skirted their question about an asking price with a request that they just make an offer. "I just need to settle Mother's estate and wouldn't mind traveling a bit. I'm not looking to get rich. I'm just looking for someone to love the home I grew up in." Dexter wanted to take everything into consideration and make the *right* kind of offer though. He didn't want to take advantage of the situation.

It felt good to be making decisions and planning for a future with Christina. An idea for the timeline was starting to form. If everything went smoothly, the transitions could all take place by summer. Dexter thought it would be wonderful to set their wedding date for the anniversary of their first date. There were still a lot of ifs, he knew…. But it was food for thought.

Christina's voice pulled him out of his thoughts. "What do you think about renting a storage unit during the transition? And beyond if we need it."

"Yeah, we'll probably almost have to," he said, thinking of all the items he didn't know what to do with. And he hadn't even gotten to furniture yet.

"I'll need to store a lot of my things to make room for Jordan and Brianna to start moving in."

"Will you and Payton stay there until everything is squared away?"

"Yeah, I think that will be okay with them. I can move into Haley's room and give them the master bedroom. Or maybe downstairs...they'll probably want to go ahead and start fixing up the nursery and might want that room."

"Will they be in a hurry to move in?"

"No I think they're thinking late spring."

"Oh, good. So you don't have to decide just yet."

"I suppose not," Christina said. "Do you think Spencer will help with some of the renovations?"

"I think so," Dexter said. "I haven't talked to him much since he got back. I wanted to give him and Paula some space to work on their relationship."

"I've talked to Paula some along and along. She has been seeing a counselor too, and I think it's going well. She says it's such a relief to actually talk about it and let go of the shame and secrecy. They're going to start couples therapy soon and probably do that retreat she mentioned."

"I'm glad," he said, meaning it. "And either way, I can get a crew together to help. It's all actually very doable."

"Let's pray on it while we get appraisals and weigh everything out," Christina suggested. "If it's meant to be, God will pave the way."

Dexter agreed. He could just see little ones playing in that backyard! And Titus! Dexter would love to see him well enough to come for a visit. When he and Christina had visited last month, the boy looked so much better, so much stronger than he had at Christmas. He and Christina continued to pray fervently for his complete recovery. The child had been added to the prayer list of every church they had visited with their mission report, so he knew lots of prayers were going up on his behalf. He made a mental note to reach out to Ruth for an update soon.

~~~~~~~~~~

Spring was a season of rebirth and renewal, and that's precisely how the season felt to Dexter. After having all the properties in question appraised, Dexter and Christina made an offer on the farmhouse, which Annie accepted without hesitation. There would be a sale to clear the house of its contents later in the month, and then Dexter and whoever he could get to help him would begin working on the siding and floors. Meanwhile, he and Christina worked on getting their respective houses in order and making loose plans for a summer wedding. It felt like a new beginning in so many ways.

Dexter put off getting in touch with Sarah as long as he could, but really needed to know what to do with some of the things they shared. He tapped out a text message asking her to call him when she had time. Her call came within thirty minutes. Dexter explained that he was going to be moving and that he wondered if she would want some of the things he had come across.

"Like what?" Sarah asked.

"Like the bedding in the hall closet that has never been used and some household items. They're all new," he said. "Maybe you had bought them for gifts."

"Nah, just donate them or whatever."

"There were some photo albums too."

In the beat of silence that followed, Dexter imagined her mind trying to register the albums and then trying to determine the best response. They couldn't deny their history, but they both had new loves. There weren't even any children to hold onto them for. "I don't know," she finally answered. "I don't want them just thrown out."

"Yeah," he said, not adding more. He understood.

"I'll take them," she said.

"Okay, cool," Dexter replied. "Want to meet at Beth's tomorrow? I'll bring them to you."

"Sure. So you're moving?"

"Yes, I'm getting married. Christina and I wanted a fresh start. We're selling both houses and buying a farmhouse just outside of town."

"Congratulations, Dexter," she said quietly. "I'm happy for you." She sounded sincere.

"Thank you. It feels good to be happy again."

They hung up, and Dexter delivered the albums as promised, surprising Sarah by not sitting down to catch up at Beth's. He did offer to buy her a coffee to go, but she declined. Instead, he ordered his favorite as well as Christina's. He was heading to her house next to take a swatch of exterior paint samples. The old weatherboard siding turned out to be in decent shape, but would need to be scraped and repainted.

Paint swatches tucked under his arm, Dexter carried the coffees to Christina's front door. His hands were full, but he managed to ring the doorbell. The door opened and Dexter looked up expecting to see his fiancé's beautiful face. Instead, he was standing face to face with Spencer.

Dexter could only imagine the myriad of emotions that flitted over his face. After all the months of trying to avoid Christina being alone with Spencer, and here he was *in her house.* Spencer rescued him from having to decide whether to punch him in the nose or give him the benefit of the doubt by saying, "Dex, I'm glad it's you. You're next on my list." Spencer stepped back to let Dexter in the door.

Christina emerged from the kitchen, drying her hands. "Oh, Dex," she said with a smile. She rushed over to take the coffee from him and give him a kiss. "We were just talking about you."

Dexter offered an uncertain smile. "I didn't know anyone else was here or I'd have brought coffee all around."

"I have a pot brewing so maybe they won't suffer too badly," Christina said. "Mmm… this *is* a treat though! Thank you."

"They…?"

"Paula's in the kitchen. Come on in."

Dexter felt relief flood through him, with guilt quick on its heels. He felt so bad that he didn't trust his brother alone with his fiancé. But Spencer had given him plenty of reasons not to trust him. He laid the paint samples down and followed Christina into the kitchen. The four of them sat down to coffee and conversation.

"It's kind of like the 12 steps program that alcoholics use to stay sober," Spencer said, obviously continuing a discussion that had begun before Dexter's arrival. "A big part of it is being accountable to someone, a sponsor. And it's important to make amends with people you've wronged." He looked at Dexter and then Christina. "That's why I'm here."

Christina met Dexter's eyes with a reluctant smile. Without words, she seemed to say, "let's just hear him out."

Spencer went on. "Christina, I hope you'll forgive me for the way I treated you. I realize that I disrespected you, and I disrespected Anthony's memory." He glanced at his wife, adding, "Not to mention my own wife, and my own brother." He shifted his gaze to Dexter briefly. "To say that it was a compulsion sounds too easy, like I'm not taking ownership of my actions. It *was* a compulsion, but I had been too stubborn to seek help and hadn't figured out ways to control my impulses. I'm learning strategies now that will help me to do the right thing."

"Of course, I forgive you," Christina said sincerely, casting a smile toward Paula.

"And Dexter, my baby brother," Spencer began with a sigh, "I haven't been much of an example to you. Thank God you've always been a better man than I have."

Dexter leaned back in his chair, not sure what to say. He just held his gaze on Spencer, encouraging him to continue. "I'm sorry to have let you down in that way. I'm sorry that I wasn't a better example, and I'm sorry that I didn't honor your relationship with Christina. I could understand if you never wanted to acknowledge me as your brother again… but Dex, I hope you can forgive me."

Dexter wanted to believe the best, and he was certain that he saw sincerity in his big brother's face. "It's like it never happened," Dexter said. When a relieved smile began to spread across Spencer's face, Dexter quickly added, "but it better *never*. Happen. Again."

"I'm doing everything within my power to manage this thing so that I won't make the same mistakes again," Spencer said.

"Then I'm proud of you," Dexter said. "Hold your head up and do your best every day. Now you have tools in your toolbelt and God at your side. Mistakes are mistakes. They don't have to define you."

"Thank you." Tears formed in Spencer's eyes, as he was obviously overcome with appreciation for the mercy that could only be the mark of true Christians. "Thank you both for not letting the worst in me make you lose sight of the man I mean to be."

Chapter Twenty-two

They were blessed with exceptionally good weather as spring officially arrived. Dexter noticed every new bud and listened with new interest to every bird song because Christina shared them with him. Her love of the season caused him to love it. He thought she had never been more beautiful than when she discovered lilies emerging or rosebuds adorning a bush that was dormant the previous month. It was like watching a child at Christmas!

It was especially delightful to witness the spring awakening on their new property. Christina rolled up her sleeves and pulled up carpet, painted, laid tile, buffed floors, and did anything else that needed to be done. But every day included a walk around the yard to check for new signs of life. And it seemed that every day brought something new -- peony bushes pushing up through the hard ground, creeping phlox covering a bank, a cluster of lilies at the edge of the property. They were so happy to be discovering it together.

Those weeks unrolled with a spirit of hope and discovery. Dexter and Christina spent long days working on creating a home in which to begin their marital journey. Spencer and several of Dexter's buddies pitched in, and by May, the house was transformed. Christina had chosen a creamy pale yellow for the exterior paint. White wicker furniture and two swings boasted blue cushions on the porch. Azaleas bloomed along the driveway and the front of the house. Hardwood floors had been buffed to a shine and adorned with rugs. Lighting had been replaced in the kitchen, and new under-cabinet added. Many rooms had received fresh coats of paint. The front door wore a large "B" and showed proudly through the new full-length glass storm door. Little by little they brought in pieces of furniture and other items from each of their current homes, merging to create an atmosphere that represented both of them.

Dexter was pleased with the progress they had made and was ready to firm up plans for their marriage. If all went well, he had a surprise up his sleeve. June 10th was the Saturday closest to the anniversary of their first date... a mere month away. They had made good progress though, and their home would be ready to move into. Could he persuade Christina to become his bride sooner rather than later? He planned to try!

~~~~~~~~~~~

"That's only a month away," Haley said.

"Yes, but..."Christina began.

"Mom, you know how weddings are... even when you think they're going to be small."

Christina was wavering -- Dexter could see it. He should have used the strategy he used when he proposed and got the children on board first. Now he was going to have to convince Haley just like he had convinced Christina.... And hopefully before Christina had to be convinced again!

"Weddings are what we want them to be. They don't have to extravagant," Dexter contributed.

"Dex, no offense, but you're a guy." She completely dismissed him and turned to her mother, "You know how these things grow."

Christina looked from Haley to Dexter and then back. "Then let it grow. I'm up for a challenge."

Dexter grinned. *Atta-girl!*

"Look," Christina went on, "the plan is to keep it small. No formal invitations, no dress fittings, no big decorations -- we're over all that. We just don't see any reason to wait now that the house is done."

"We could have been planning the whole time," Haley said.

"But we weren't sure how long the house would take. Besides, you've seen what our clan can accomplish in a short period of time. Just look at the mission," Christina said.

Haley sighed. "That's true. Maybe it *is* do-able. But don't forget that Jared and I are moving into Dexter's place too."

That decision had been a recent development, with Haley focused on her internship practically until the end. They were going to rent for a year while establishing credit to get their credit score where it needed to be for a home loan.

"It wouldn't matter if we got married in June or September. The transition involves everyone and will be chaotic," Dexter said.

"But June is definitely preferable because of the baby," Christina said. Jordan and Brianna's little one was due in August.

"So, where's this shindig gonna go down? It might be hard to book a venue on such short notice." Haley sounded a little negative, but Dexter knew she was being practical.

He looked at Christina and grinned. She met his gaze, mirroring his grin. "The farmhouse property is looking lovely. We were thinking the backyard would be a terrific place for a wedding," Dexter explained.

Christina supplied, "Nothing fancy, but perfect for us. And we'll see if Pastor Lawrence or Pastor James is available. If they both happen to be, they can co-officiate."

Haley smiled broadly. "Okay, then. Sounds like we're about to have a wedding!"

Christina beamed and then turned sincere. "Oh, and Haley-bug…" She stepped forward and took her daughter's hands, "Will you be my matron-of-honor?"

Haley squeezed her mother's hands and touched her forehead to hers. "Of course, I will."

That left Dexter thinking about his best man. Spencer had stood up with him when he married Sarah, and being his only brother, seemed an obvious choice. After all that had gone down between him and Christina though, Dexter just wasn't sure it was the right thing. He put that decision on the backburner. God would provide an answer.

On that fine May afternoon, as Christina and Haley left to accompany Brianna to her OB appointment, Dexter shifted his focus to a project that he hoped Christina would love. To do it up right, there wouldn't be much of a way to surprise her with it. But he sure wished he could. The beautiful white gazebo he planned to erect could be instrumental in the wedding and also serve as his wedding gift to her. Actually… *Wonder if I could build it somewhere else and then move it?* He made a couple of calls to get some input from some construction friends, one of whom offered a space to work on it as well as to help move it when it was completed. Maybe he *could* surprise her after all!

Dexter ordered the materials from a local hardware store, effectively setting the plan in motion. He could pour the concrete foundation a few days prior to the wedding and then move it in and get it secured when Christina wasn't around. She was going to love this!

~~~~~~~~~~

Dexter looked down at his phone screen. The message from Ruth should be terrific news, but something seemed a little odd about her end of the correspondence lately. And Lisa had been positively avoiding him, he was sure of it. With only two weeks until the wedding, he just wanted confirmation that Titus and his family would be there. Lisa had said only that they would be there if they could. He hadn't spoken directly to Titus in weeks, but he thought about him every day and continued to pray for the boy's health. The last two times he had mentioned a facetime visit, Lisa had said that it wasn't a good time. And now Ruth's message left him feeling... well, *dismissed.*

Ty is doing quite well now. Thanks for all your prayers.

Normally Titus' grandmother was very friendly and made Dexter feel like an old friend, if not a member of the family. But that's not how he was feeling lately. He tapped out a reply.

Great! I hope to see all of you at the wedding.

Ruth neither confirmed nor declined, but simply indicated that it had been nice talking with him. Dexter was confused and disappointed. Maybe they just clung to Christina's and his faith when things were precarious with Titus. Maybe he and Christina had served their purpose and no longer had a place in their lives. Dexter knew he had been guilty of that before -- not recognizing when it was time for a season of friendship to fade.

He sighed, reminding himself that the main thing was that Titus' health had improved tremendously. He whispered his thanks to God for that and tried to focus on the tasks at hand. The gazebo was coming along nicely, but it was getting harder to explain his lack of available time to Christina. She had no idea of this undertaking and he was afraid she was starting to feel like he wasn't willing to do his part with all the loose ends that needed to be tied up. Jordan, Payton, and Jared were stepping up to help with all the moving. They were privy to the surprise and helped smooth things over with Christina. Still, his absence had to be conspicuous.

After working all day, putting in three hours of work on the gazebo, and grabbing supper from a drive-thru, Dexter entered his house feeling exhausted and defeated. He should be proud of the progress on the gazebo, but he couldn't shake the feeling that something was amiss with Titus' family. Maybe he wasn't the important part of their lives that he thought. And with little time to spend with Christina the past few days, his perspective was a little skewed. It was amazing how she set things right with his world, and her absence threw him off balance. His house was bare and dismal. Dexter was so ready to have these next two weeks behind him so he could come home to Christina instead.

He plugged his dead phone in to charge while he scarfed down his food and took a shower. He would call Christina afterward, and that would make him feel better. Dexter's house had few furnishings at this point, as many of his belongings had taken up residence at the farmhouse already. The bedroom was intact, however. He emerged from the shower and went to retrieve lounge pants from the dresser. When he pulled out his last clean pair (*must do laundry*), the pile of small parcels that remained from Christina's Christmas gift was revealed. It had been a while since he had opened one. As he sifted through the pile, the one that said "For when you've had a bad day" caught his eye. Had he had a bad day? It felt *bad* at that moment, but he was tired. The day had been productive. The only bad thing that had happened, aside from not seeing Christina, was his frustrating correspondence with Ruth. And that may have only been his perception. Still, it had left him feeling...well, bad.

And then another little package demanded his attention. "For when you doubt yourself," it read. That seemed like the right one for tonight. Dexter picked it up and gently untied the ribbon that bound it. He opened the flap on the envelope, finding the words *You are loved* and little hand-drawn hearts and flowers before he even got to the folded note inside. He smiled at Christina's thoughtfulness. He unfolded the contents of the envelope.

Proverbs 3:5,6 Trust in the Lord with all thine heart and <u>lean not unto thine own understanding</u>. In all thy ways, acknowledge Him and He shall direct thy paths.

Don't forget, my love, that we don't have the big picture. A strand of thread has no idea of its priceless contribution to a beautiful tapestry because it doesn't have the proper view. But the creator knows because the creator sees! Don't doubt that God has you where He wants you and that even when it doesn't feel like it, YOU ARE IMPORTANT. We don't have to understand the part we play as long as we trust in Him.

Dexter wept at this precious reminder, which was precisely what he needed. Between the note and his subsequent conversation with Christina, he felt the weight fall away from his shoulders. His perspective shifted back into place. Christina assured him that he was reading too much into Ruth's clipped tone, that the older woman was probably just busy. She recounted progress that had been made at the farmhouse -- new curtains had been hung, new bedding had arrived for the bedroom suite they purchased from Annie, items she and Paula had found at Target were going to look beautiful, and so on. Dexter tried to reciprocate, but most of his progress couldn't be revealed because it was a surprise. Instead, he tried to get a feel for where her efforts would be the next couple of weeks. He shared his plans to work on lighting the following week, indicating a need for the power to be shut off. This was not a lie. He did indeed plan to work on lighting...including lighting in the new gazebo.

"I was hoping you'd be finished with most of the work you're doing so I wouldn't be a bother to you while we're trying to get that done."

"We should have everything in order by the weekend. I think you will be pleased with how it's looking. Just stay away if you can, and that way you'll get the full effect all at once."

Dexter could hear her excitement. "I can't wait to see it," he said, meaning it. "I shouldn't have to be out there for anything until the beginning of next week."

"The beginning of our *wedding week*," she squealed.

"It's finally almost here," he said, smiling, feeling loads better than he had an hour before.

"I can hardly wait! In just a matter of days, I'll be Mrs. Dexter Billings!"

Chapter Twenty-three

The days slid by as days will do. The weather had cooperated, and Dexter had been able to finish the gazebo and was planning to pour a quick-set concrete foundation as soon as Christina was off the premises. He had his fingers crossed that the weather would hold and he would be able to move the gazebo in on Friday before the rehearsal dinner. Meanwhile, his fiance was chomping at the bit to show him all the finishing touches she and the girls had put on the house.

Dexter had been so busy that he hadn't even seen the property in almost two weeks. In that length of time, lilies and rosebushes had bloomed. Heavy pink peonies kissed the ground. The air was fragrant and the landscape was colorful. He was dazzled before he even went inside. Honestly, it was hard to walk past the inviting front porch and leave it all behind. Christina had added splashes of color with throw pillows on the porch furniture and several large flower pots brimming with flowers of every color. She pulled him along though, and they stepped inside the door.

Dexter's breath caught. He had thought it looked nice when he was here before. But now! Christina had hung pictures on the walls, accented with carefully placed sconces and shelves. On the wall adjacent to the fireplace, a beautiful shelf with a dowel rod held a striking double wedding ring quilt suspended so that it hovered just above the baseboard. "Where did *that* come from?" Dexter asked, ogling the quilt.

"That was my grandmother's, made by her mother as a wedding gift. It has been in my possession for a while, but I had it packed away. I kind of feel like it needed some air… and that we needed to enjoy it."

"It is gorgeous! Are you sure? We wouldn't want anything to happen to it."

"I don't either, but what good is it packed away?" she said.

"It looks great in that spot. *Everything* looks great!"

"You've not even seen it all yet! Come on." She tugged him eagerly through the rest of the house, pointing out different accessories and additions. There were decorative towels, rugs, window treatments, lamps, vases of flowers, pictures on the walls… things he didn't give much thought to, but was amazed at how much cozier it made the house feel. Christina had added her touch to the place, turning their house into a home.

"I just can't get over it!" he said when the tour was complete. "It doesn't even look like the same place!"

Christina beamed under the praise, thrilled that he liked it. "Oh, I almost forgot!" She led him to the basement, where she had scrubbed it clean and brought in a dehumidifier. Its potential already shone.

Dexter was absolutely blown away by the transformation. Walking back outside, he commented, "There are so many flowers around here that I don't think we'll even need any more decorations for the wedding."

"No, we have plenty. Paula and Melissa are going to help me make some little arrangements for the tables from whatever is in bloom at the end of the week."

He agreed that that would be perfect. He pointed out places where he wanted to run lights and add outdoor ceiling fans to the porch. "Ooh, fancy!" she said, and then, "Well, I'll be out of your hair. I'm going to focus on helping Jordan and Brianna this week. Brianna keeps trying to do too much, and we have to keep that grand-daughter of ours safe!"

Dexter's heart melted when she referred to the baby as *their* grand-daughter. He pulled her into his arms and imparted a slow, sweet kiss. Minutes seemed to pass before he stepped back and looked into her eyes. "I am *so* blessed, Christina. Thank you for agreeing to share your life with me."

Christina offered a misty smile. "Less than a week!" she said.

"It can't get here fast enough."

~~~~~~~~~~

As soon as Christina left, Dexter called in his crew and they got the form set up and the concrete poured. Over the next couple of days, an electrician buddy of his was able to help out with some wiring so that a chandelier could be hung in the gazebo for the ceremony. They could replace it with something more practical afterward. By Thursday, Dexter had three ceiling fans suspended over the covered porch and some string lights put up for the festivities. More were on standby for the gazebo once it was secured. That was due to happen early the next morning, but for the moment he had done everything that could be done.

He sat down on the porch of his new home and just enjoyed the view. He tapped out a message to Christina to see if there was anything he needed to help her with, but she was good. She suggested that he check with Blair and Paula since they were providing the meal for the rehearsal dinner. He did, but they declined his help as well. Next, he tapped out a message to Lisa in an effort to ascertain whether they were going to be able to come. He waited, but there was no reply at all. Disappointment clouded his heart, but he tried not to let it take root. It was going to be a joyous time, regardless of which guests could make it.

Dexter took advantage of the solitude by approaching the throne of his Heavenly Father in prayer. *Lord, I thank You for bringing Christina into my life. I ask Your blessing on our marriage. Help me to be the man she needs me to be. Help me to be a good spiritual leader. Father, I recognize Your hand in so many aspects of my life and my relationships. It overwhelms me sometimes to see how You work things out for us. Let me never fail to acknowledge You and to give You credit for all the good and perfect gifts You bless us with. Lord, I pray for sweet Titus. I'm believing You for complete healing. I praise You for Your healing power and thank You for restoring him to health. And dear God, please be with Spencer as he journeys toward recovery. I claim him as Your child, purchased by the blood of Jesus, and ask that You bind the hands of the enemy as Spencer strives to do the right thing. Be with Paula as well, Lord. I can't imagine what this must have been like for her. Now, if it be Your will, Father -- just one more thing -- I pray that the weather will hold until our ceremony is over. In Jesus' sweet name, amen.*

~~~~~~~~~

At 6:30 a.m. the gazebo began its journey to its destination. It went smoothly, and was secured into place by midmorning. Dexter worked to hang the chandelier and add strands of clear party lights in a tasteful configuration. When he was finished, it looked magical. Satisfied with a job well done, he left to meet Christina for lunch at Beth's Bistro. They planned to pick up their wedding bands afterward.

Over two chicken salad sandwiches, Dexter asked, "So, what does the rest of the afternoon hold for you?"

"I'm going load down my car with clothes from my closet and get those put away at our new home," she said. "One of us will need to be there to help set up tables for the dinner, so I might as well go on out."

"I want to be there when you go, so will you let me know when you're heading that direction?"

She considered him, a smile spreading slowly across her face. "O-kaay….why?"

"Because I have something to show you," he said, matching her smile.

"What is it?"

"I can't tell you. It's a surprise." When she didn't answer right away, he arched an eyebrow and waited.

"Okay, I'll text you when I'm leaving home," she finally agreed.

They finished their lunch and walked down to the jewelry store to pick up their rings. When they parted, Dexter followed suit and went home to load up as many of his belongings as he had time to before Christina's text. His truck was pretty full by the time Christina's message came through. Thirty minutes later he was waiting for her when she pulled into the driveway of their home.

Dexter met her at the vehicle and walked her up onto the porch, shielding her from seeing the backyard prematurely. He pulled a bandana from his jeans pocket and fashioned a blindfold out of it. As he secured it, she giggled a little and said, "I have a surprise for you too."

"Oh yeah?"

"Mm hmm."

"When do I get to see it?" he asked.

"Depends. If I'm not impressed with whatever you've got going here, I may send it back," she teased.

Dexter led her carefully down the back steps and into the yard. "Hopefully that won't be a problem," he said. He positioned himself in front of her so he was in her line of vision as he removed the makeshift blindfold. He smiled down at her. "Are you ready to see?"

Christina nodded and Dexter stepped aside. He knew when her eyes landed on the gazebo because she gasped and clasped her hands over her mouth. She made several stabs at forming words, but to no avail. He laughed. Finally she managed, "When? How did you...? It's beautiful!"

"Come on," he said, taking her hand and pulling her up the steps.

Standing in the center of the gazebo, she turned around and around. She gasped again when she spied the chandelier.

"That isn't the permanent fixture," he explained. "That's just for the ceremony. So are the other lights. You'll be able to see them better when it gets dark."

"Oh, Dex... I love it! I love it so much!" She threw her arms around him and kissed his face and lips and nose and chin in rapid succession. "I love *you* so much!"

"So....I can't tell. Do you like it or not?" he teased.

Christina swatted him playfully and kissed him again. She rested her arms on his shoulders, her fingers playing in his hair. They kissed, and they swayed. They danced to the melody of true love, a melody that could only be heard by them. Dexter felt he could be happy living in that moment forever.

He thought he heard a car door at a distance and started to turn around, but Christina was obviously not finished with their moment. And that was okay with him. "It's probably just the food starting to arrive," she muttered, kissing him again. He kissed her back, enjoying having her in his arms.

Christina pulled back a bit, but held his gaze. "What did you and Spencer decide? Is he going to be your best man?"

"He said he could, but didn't seem thrilled about it. I think he understood that everything was still too fresh and that I had reservations about it."

"Well…. What if he just signed the license, but someone else stood up with you?"

What? What an odd… "What do you mean? Like who?" he asked.

Christina dropped her arms and stepped back. "It's just an idea," she said, grinning at him. She lifted her arm and pointed behind him.

Dexter turned to see five people walking toward them. It was his turn to gasp. The moment he had turned around, Titus broke into a run (*a run!*) and stopped only in Dexter's arms. Tears fell without warning, splashing onto the boy's shoulder as Dexter held him. "You have no idea how happy I am to see you!"

"This is your new place?" Titus asked.

"Yep. What do you think?"

"I like it!"

By then, the rest of the family caught up. They exchanged loving greetings. Dexter quickly surmised that the recent aloofness could be attributed to the surprise. And then he remembered what Christina had said about Spencer signing the license as witness while someone else stood in as best man. Suddenly, it all made perfect sense! Titus couldn't sign the paper since he was underage, but the child would likely be thrilled to have a part in the ceremony.

He looked at the amazingly healthy-looking boy. "Ty, what would you think about being my best man in the wedding?"

"What would I have to do?"

"It's an important job. You'd have to hold onto the ring. You'd stand next to me and help me be calm."

"Sure!" he said exuberantly.

"Awesome!" Dexter said, giving Titus a high five. He looked over the child's head at the adults. "Thank you for coming."

Ruth stepped forward and hugged Dexter. "We wouldn't have missed this for the world." She turned around and looked at Jack and Lisa. "Should we give them their wedding gift now?"

Lisa grinned. "Definitely." She looked around at Talia, who sat on Christina's lap. "Talia, you want to tell them?"

The little girl became very serious, thinking before she spoke. "He's inermission."

"Did she say...?" Dexter asked, hoping against hope that she was saying what he thought she was saying.

Lisa nodded happily. "I just got off the phone with the doctor about thirty miles back. According to the latest test results, Titus is officially in remission!"

A chorus of squeals and delirious laughter rose as they all hugged and bounced with excitement and praise for answered prayers. Dexter didn't think life could possibly get any better than it was right then! But of course it did. This was only the beginning.

Spencer and Paula, followed closely by Blair, arrived shortly after the raucous celebration in the gazebo. The three of them toted food into the kitchen and then, with help from Dexter and Jack, got four long folding tables set up and outfitted with chairs. Haley and Brianna breezed in with tablecloths and centerpieces. The rest of Christina's family arrived, as well as both pastors. Rehearsal went smoothly, due partly to the fact that everyone was eager to eat!

Titus and Talia were the life of the party. Everyone was charmed by the beautiful little girl who proclaimed her brother to be "inermission." By the end of the evening, Ty's family felt like their own family. If anyone there had questioned Dexter's connection with the boy and his family, they didn't by the time it was over. It was a joy to see Titus up and about and looking so well. If Dexter hadn't already known, he would have never guessed how much of the past year the child had spent in the hospital. Titus asked a lot of questions about the ring and what he should do if this or that happened. He took his responsibilities very seriously, and was bound to make a fabulous best man.

A meal of baked ham, potato salad, green beans and rolls rewarded their efforts to rehearse. As the sun set and daylight faded, Dexter turned on the festive lights. Paula made coffee, and Blair brought out banana pudding and strawberry pie. *What a wonderful evening!* Dexter thought, surrounded by all the love and laughter. He hated to see it end, but alas, it did.

Ty's family had a room at a nearby hotel. They were among the first to leave, with Dexter promising to come swim with Titus and Talia the next day if there was time.

"It's his wedding day," Lisa admonished. "He may not have time for swimming!"

"Well, the wedding isn't until 7:00, so we'll see. I might could work it in," Dexter said with a wink in Ty's direction.

He mentioned it to Christina later, after they had been shooed away so that Paula and Blair could clean up without them underfoot. Dexter sat with his soon-to-be bride on one of the porch swings, swaying gently to and fro. He delighted in the knowledge that evenings filled with this activity were part of his new *normal*.

"What all do we have to accomplish tomorrow?" he asked.

"Well, I think one of the deacons is going to bring more tables and chairs at some point, but Melissa assures me that they'll get them all set up. Payton is picking up the cake tomorrow afternoon. Lily wants to take me to get my nails done."

"What do I need to do? Titus wants me to come swim at the hotel pool, but it's hard to imagine kicking back like that on our wedding day!"

"I think kicking back is exactly what you need to do. And I do too. We've earned it!"

"Would you like to come swimming?" he asked, amused.

"Nah, my kicking back will be in the form of a mani/pedi and picking flowers for a bouquet."

He grinned and kissed her temple. "Okay then, what time do I need to be here?"

"Well, how do you feel about us seeing each other before the wedding?"

"Honestly? I've always thought the bad luck thing was a little silly."

"Great! I don't believe in that stuff either. My God is bigger than superstition. This means we can get pictures beforehand. Maybe about 4:00?"

"I can do that," he said. He was quiet for a moment and then, "So, you loved the gazebo?"

"I did! And was so surprised! Did you do all that this week?"

"I had been working on it somewhere else for a while, and just moved it here this week."

"Amazing! I love it. Thank you for being so thoughtful."

"Me thoughtful? What about all the thought it took to get my little best man here without me knowing?"

Christina laughed. "They all wanted to surprise you, so it wasn't that hard. The hardest part was seeing your hurt and confusion over their cool responses."

"It all makes sense now," Dexter said.

The couple sat there swinging and talking until long after the others had left. Christina intimated, "You know, I'd be just as happy to stay right here in our new home tomorrow night if it wasn't for everyone else being here."

"Yeah, we don't want our big exit to be excusing ourselves to the bedroom!" They both laughed at that. "I have reservations for just a couple of nights at a place you'll like. I'm like you… just eager to be in our own home, starting our new life."

Their parting was reluctant, but made bearable by the knowledge that it would be the last time.

~~~~~~~~~~

Dexter slept in and then laid out his suit and checked the ring and marriage license before driving to the hotel to spend time with Titus and Talia. He spent a big chunk of the day there, enjoying the visit with all the family. Dexter was amazed when he stepped out of the shower that afternoon and realized that he would need to head directly on to the farmhouse once he dressed. He had feared that the day would drag by like it would for a kid waiting for a birthday to arrive. It hadn't. Dexter pulled into the driveway at 3:50, and the next three hours went by in a blur.

The first hour and a half was filled with photographing his family and then Christina's family. And then the photographer, a friend of Blair's, wanted to capture his first glimpse of his bride. Dexter played along, but thought it was a little pretentious for a second go-round.

He stood on the steps of the gazebo, dutifully looking in the other direction while Christina approached from behind. Following directions, Dexter didn't respond when he felt Christina's hand on his shoulder. He heard the rapid fire of the camera from his left and was then given permission to turn around slowly. He pivoted counterclockwise, his eyes landing on Christina.

That was when the world fell away and left only him and Christina. Dexter had never seen her look lovelier. The dress she wore hugged her beautiful body in all the right places and then flowed gracefully down from her waist, brushing her legs in a very fetching manner. The color of the dress -- what would Blair call that? Cream? Ivory? -- made her summer skin look like his favorite chai tea. A shy coral graced her lips, which were curved into a radiant, sincere smile. A deeper coral touched her fingertips and the toes peeking out from her open-toed shoes. In her hands was a bouquet of flowers he recognized from their yard, mostly lilies. Dexter drank her in completely.

Eventually, aspects of the real world returned. He heard the click of the camera. Voices nearby. The trees and the house filling the background behind Christina. But still, he couldn't take his eyes off her. He was aware of other things, other people… but none of it mattered. Nothing mattered except her. Nothing was more important than the fact that he was about to make her his wife.

The intensity of his stare made Christina blush and dip her head. She looked up at him sweetly as she drew closer. "You're not going to back out on me, are you?" she said, reaching up to smooth his lapel.

"Not a chance!" He placed a hand on the small of her back, drawing her closer, intending to kiss her.

Christina stopped him with a palm against his chest. "No kissing until you put a ring on it, mister!"

He looked at his watch impatiently. "Then let's get this show on the road," he said.

She laughed. "It isn't quite time yet. Our guests would be mighty disappointed, arriving only to find out we had jumped the gun!"

"I guess you're right. I've waited my whole life for you; what's another…" He looked at his watch again. "…40 minutes?"

"That's the spirit!"

The pair posed for a few more pictures as guests began to arrive. Everyone mingled around the yard, admiring the flowers and decorations. Before he knew it, it was time for them to take their places. Dexter, Christina, their families, Pastor James, Pastor Lawrence, and Titus all assembled on the porch. Haley reached up and rang the bell that normally called folks to dinner. Today it signified the beginning. The guests began to find seats. As Rascal Flatts' "Bless the Broken Road" began to play over a Bluetooth speaker, the pastors made their way to the gazebo and everyone but the actual wedding party filed in and took seats near the front. Finally, Dexter joined the pastors on the gazebo while Titus walked with Haley down the aisle. They waited on either side of the steps, turning when a saxophone belted the notes of "The Wedding March." The entire audience rose to its feet and watched with rapt attention as Christina walked down the aisle and stepped up into the gazebo. Titus and Haley stepped up into their places then, and the music faded.

Pastor James stepped forward with an open Bible and read a passage from the second chapter of Genesis, speaking briefly about how God created both man and woman because it was "not good for man to be alone." He stepped aside and made room for Pastor Lawrence, who led Dexter and Christina in the exchange of their vows and rings. Titus fumbled a little while retrieving Christina's ring. This elicited a nervous round of chuckles from the wedding party. The boy produced it though, and Dexter proudly slipped it onto Christina's finger.

Mere moments after it began, Dexter was given permission to kiss his bride. And he did. Ever so gently, he cupped Christina's face in his hands and looked into her eyes. The photographer let out a not-so-subtle *ahem*, and Dexter promptly dropped a hand down to Christina's upper arm so as not to obstruct anyone's view. He leaned in and touched his lips to hers. Dexter tried not to abandon tact, but couldn't resist deepening the kiss possessively just for a moment. She was finally his!

Somewhere beyond the elation that permeated his being, Dexter heard Pastor Lawrence.

"Ladies and gentlemen, it is my pleasure to present to you *Mr. and Mrs. Dexter Billings.*"

Epilogue

The Christmas tree twinkled in the corner of the room, a fire crackling nearby. The entire first floor of the house was filled with the scent of cider and gingerbread. It was their third Christmas at the farmhouse. New traditions had been started, and today's was one of Dexter's favorites. Paula, Blair, Haley, Brianna, and Lily joined Christina for a day of baking and candy-making. Dexter embraced his role as "Papa" by helping Jordan and Jared keep their tots occupied and out of the kitchen. Jordan and Brianna's daughter, Aria, was just old enough to be enchanted by all the lights and festivities. She sat in Dexter's lap, turning the pages of a storybook.

Nearby Jared and Haley's nine month old son, Liam, sat contentedly in a playpen. He banged soft plastic shapes together and babbled happily. A ballgame was on TV, but Dexter was tuned into the laughter coming from the kitchen and Liam's sweet jabbering. He couldn't be happier.

Christina called from the kitchen, "Who's ready for some cider and sausage balls?"

"That sounds good!" Spencer said.

Dexter stood and handed Aria off to her Uncle Payton with a kiss. "Let me go see if Ma needs some help."

"You have to be quiet though," Payton said. "The game's on."

Jordan snickered. "You just wait," he told his little brother. "Your time's coming."

Payton looked stricken. "How'd you know?"

Dexter paused, overhearing. He motioned Christina over.

Jordan laughed out loud. "I didn't! I was just speaking generally!"

Amused, Jared said, "Sounds like you've got some news to share."

In the kitchen, Lily wondered why everyone was suddenly looking at her. "What?"

Christina motioned her over, where Payton cast her a sheepish look. "I think I accidentally let the cat out of the bag."

Lily placed her hands on her hips. "Well, poo! We planned to surprise you on Christmas. I guess this is close enough!"

"The baby's due in June," Payton admitted with a grin.

"Dang, you guys didn't waste any time once you tied the knot, did you?!" Brianna teased from behind Lily.

Congratulations abounded. Dexter wrapped his arms around his wife, kissing the top of her head. She looked up at him. "Isn't it wonderful?"

He nodded. It was indeed wonderful, so wonderful to witness the way life goes on.

Sources of information for this work include:

National Council on Sexual Addiction and Compulsivity

DSM-4

Holy Bible

If you are so inspired, these and many other hospitals will be grateful for your donations:

www.stjude.org

www.shrinershospitals.org/Donate

https://nortonchildrens.com/donate/

Made in the USA
Lexington, KY
14 January 2018